LIFE SHADOWS

THE BARNWOOD BUILDER MYSTERIES
BOOK 1

LORI BEASLEY BRADLEY

Copyright (C) 2018 Lori Beasley Bradley

Layout design and Copyright (C) 2021 by Next Chapter

Published 2021 by Next Chapter

Mass Market Paperback Edition

This book is a work of fiction. Names, characters, places, and incidents are the product of the author's imagination or are used fictitiously. Any resemblance to actual events, locales, or persons, living or dead, is purely coincidental.

All rights reserved. No part of this book may be reproduced or transmitted in any form or by any means, electronic or mechanical, including photocopying, recording, or by any information storage and retrieval system, without the author's permission.

1

Nathan and Amelia Ryan were the heart of Barnwood Builders.

As a matter of fact, they were all of Barn-wood Builders. Nathan, a forty-year-old, out-of-work carpenter and his sister Amelia, a thirty-eight-year-old internet marketer between positions were the Barn-wood Builders.

Amelia had used a few pieces of the distressed old boards Nathan had hauled home from a barn he was tearing down with their father to make some picture frames, plaques, and small boxes which she then took to a local swap meet. They sold so well Nathan got in on the action and built some tables and stools to add to Amelia's display. They were soon seeing hundreds of dollars each weekend. Amelia expanded the business to include an online store and Barn-wood Builders had been born.

When Nathan and his father were hired to tear down an old Victorian house in Briarton, archeological salvage items such as doorknobs, moldings, and fixtures were added to the business. Amelia created plaques from embossed tin ceiling tiles or antique wallpaper framed in fancy molding material. Nathan was selling his tables, benches, bookcases, and chairs made from the recovered wood as well as the wood itself by the square foot to earn a healthy income.

"Where are we off to today, big brother?" Amelia asked as she poured her first cup of her brother's bitter coffee. He always used four scoops of grounds rather than three and made the brew too strong for Amelia's taste, but he always managed to beat her to the pot by five minutes, so she got used to drinking the strong coffee and didn't complain—much.

"An old barn north of town by that dried up old lake."

"Lake Hamilton?" she asked as she popped an everything bagel into the over-sized chrome toaster and waited for the savory aroma of onion to hit her nostrils and make her mouth water.

Nathan snorted. "Ain't much of a lake anymore," he said. "Just a mosquito-infested pond choked up with lily pads and full of poisonous water snakes. Nobody even fishes there anymore because it's such a pit."

Amelia smiled as she gingerly took the hot bagel from the toaster. "I remember Grandpa O'Connor telling me him and Grandma used to swim there when they were young and first dating. Lake Hamilton was like the make-out place to go when they were in school."

Nathan curled his lip in disgust. "I don't want to think about Grandpa and Grandma making out," he said, shaking his head of thick brown hair. "It's gross."

Amelia grinned at her sheepish brother. "How do you think Mother got here—immaculate conception?

I'm pretty certain Grandma was about three months along when they got married."

Nathan swallowed the last of his coffee and winked at Amelia. "That's my story and I'm stickin' to it." He glanced at his sister's freshly buttered bagel on a paper towel. "Bring that with you. I'm ready to roll, sis."

Amelia topped off her coffee cup, snatched up the bagel in the paper towel, and followed her brother out to his shiny new red pickup with Barn-wood Builders, Inc. and Amelia's cellphone number stenciled on the doors.

She handled all the scheduling and general business aspects of the small company, and it was doing well enough for her brother to invest in the flashy new pickup. She still drove the Subaru she'd left her marriage with.

Amelia finished her bagel and coffee as Nathan maneuvered his truck through the small town of Briarton and into the verdant green countryside. The aroma of fresh-cut hay and newly plowed fields filtered in through the truck's vent system and Amelia smiled. She'd been so eager to escape Briarton at eighteen when she'd graduated Briarton High with honors and gone off to a good state university on a full-ride scholarship. Twenty years later and she was back sleeping in her old room at her parents' house with a curfew and ready to run again.

Amelia knew she'd disappointed her mother by not living up to her potential and landing a high-powered job in corporate America somewhere. Instead Amelia had gone into business for herself as an internet marketer and had failed miserably in her mother's opinion.

After her last gig marketing for a group of independently published authors had dried up and her marriage had fallen apart, Amelia had returned to Briarton and the home of Matthew and Elizabeth Ryan—her parents. She hadn't felt too guilty because her brother Nathan had moved back in about the same time after his divorce. Neither sibling had given their parents grandchildren—another disappointment in Elizabeth's eyes.

"We're quite the pair, aren't we, sis?" Nathan said as he turned off the asphalt pavement onto a gravel road, almost sensing Amelia's thoughts.

It was something they'd both been able to do since childhood, but nothing unusual for the sensitive O'-Connor side of the family.

"Why," Amelia smirked, "because we're both a couple of out-of-work, divorced adult losers living at home again with their poor parents?"

"Hey now," Nathan said with a chuckle. "They're not so poor since we've been kickin' in several hundred a month from what Mom calls our silly little hobby business."

Amelia smiled as she emptied her cup of coffee before Nathan could slosh it all over her on the bumpy old road. "Yah," she said with a sigh, "a four-year degree from one of the best schools in the state, and I make fucking picture frames and trinket boxes in my dad's garage."

Nathan grinned. "Fucking picture frames and trinket boxes that sell like hot cakes." He reached across the seat to take his sister's hand. "We've got nothing to be ashamed of, sis. We may be living back at home with our parents, but we're not freeloading.

We're paying our way, and you should be proud of that."

Amelia put her other hand atop her brother's. "I am, Bubba," she said with a sigh, "I am, but I'm getting tired of Mom's sideways glances and snide remarks. She's getting on my last nerve and I'm tired of it." She saw the ravaged roof of an old barn up ahead through the trees. "Is that it?"

"Yep." Nathan turned off the rutted track and parked in tall grass in front of the weathered old barn. "Doesn't she look great?" He sounded enthusiastic and Amelia smiled. "The owner said we could have anything we found inside. This could be a real gold mine, sis. Just look at the colors on that wood."

Amelia studied the faded paint on the leaning structure with the open wagon area stuffed with rusted farm equipment, old screened doors, and mouse-eaten furniture. She wished she could see what her brother saw with such enthusiasm. "It looks more like a death-trap to me," she said, "I bet the next big wind could blow it over."

"That's what ol' man Mathers is afraid of," her brother said, "and why he wants it torn down before some kid gets hurt out here nosin' through it during Summer break." Nathan opened his door. "Let's go have a look but watch out for snakes. The old man said the place is crawlin' with 'em because of the mice and bats inside."

"Great, mice, bats, and snakes. You take me to the nicest places, big brother." Amelia got out of the truck and waded through the tall green weeds, swaying in the warm May breeze. Amelia made her way to the opposite end of the barn from her brother, where she'd seen an old door hanging open. Something told her the interesting stuff would be in there and Amelia always listened to her hunches. It was something her grandmother had impressed upon her at an early age.

"You have the family gift, child," Jenny O'Connor had told her granddaughter during one of her rare visits to Lockwood Asylum with her grandfather before his death. "Always listen to your inner voice." Jenny had tapped Amelia's temple. "It will never steer you wrong, child."

As Amelia neared the old door made from eight-inch silver-gray planks held together by four-inch boards nailed together in the shape of a Z, she heard the sound of a girl weeping and hoped her inner voice hadn't sent her on a lark. Amelia glanced around outside the old barn but didn't see anyone. Who would be hanging out in this old rat trap?

Amelia felt the hairs on the back of her neck lift off her skin as she yanked on the old door and peeked inside the dark room. The raised hairs on her arms was never a good sign. She smelled damp, moldy hay from the loft, and the acrid scent of rodents and their droppings. She glanced around the dark room for snakes. Where there were rodents, Amelia knew there would be snakes. Thistle and wild mustard grew from the dirt floor around the rotted bottom of the old walls where some sunlight seeped through. It looked like every old barn Amelia had ever been inside.

The sound of weeping grew stronger as she stepped inside the dark space, and the tiny hairs on her arms stood up as if drawn by electricity in the air from a thunderstorm. Amelia's heart thudded in her chest, and she flinched with a muffled yelp when barn-swallows swooped from their mud nests on the rafters to fly out the door above her head. She waited for a snake to fall and drape around her shoulders the way one always did in the old horror movies. She breathed a sigh of relief when none did and stepped with confidence deeper into the dark space.

"Is someone there?" Amelia called. "Do you need help?"

Amelia's eyes were drawn to a blue glow materializing upon a platform built about six or eight inches off the dirt floor of the old barn. It looked to be an old feeding station for dairy cows. Amelia was no farm girl, but she'd grown up in farm country and recognized the slots where the cows would have been led to eat while being milked. She stepped closer and felt that electric buzz in the air lift the hairs on the back of her neck this time.

Seeing a glowing apparition might have sent most sane people running for their life, but this was nothing new to Amelia. Her grandmother, Jenny O'-Connor, called them Life Shadows and Amelia had been seeing them since her first period at age twelve. Her grandmother had explained they were the energy left behind by a person who couldn't move on to the next plane for some reason—usually a violent death or the refusal to accept they were, in truth, dead. She wondered what had happened to this poor girl to keep her stuck in this nasty old barn.

Grandma Jenny had told Amelia it was their responsibility as seers to help those trapped souls to find their way into the light when they came upon them. Jenny O'Connor had spent the majority of her adult life in a state asylum for the mentally ill because Amelia's mother refused to believe in or accept her mother's calling. Jenny embarrassed Elizabeth with her talk of communing with the dead, and Elizabeth had her mother institutionalized as soon as she was old enough to be recognized as an adult by the state.

"Who are you and what do you want?" Amelia asked with a brave step forward into the dark web-strewn room. Amelia was much more frightened of living spiders than long-dead humans and batted at the shimmering webs undulating in the room.

The girl turned to stare at Amelia with wide brown eyes in her pale bruised and bloody face. "You can see me?" the girl who wore no clothes asked. It surprised Amelia the girl didn't try to cover herself.

"Yes," Amelia replied with trembling lips. "Who are you and what are you doing here?"

Tears slid down the girl's cheeks. "I'm Peg," she answered, "and I want to go home but I can't." The girl stood and walked toward Amelia but stopped abruptly at the edge of the raised platform as if held in place by an invisible a force field. "I can't go any further than this and I want to go home to my mama so bad. It's dark and the picnic's been over for hours. She must wonder where I've got off to, and my daddy will be mad as hell and will beat her black and blue with his belt for lettin' me go on the picnic after he'd said I couldn't go because there would be boys there who might get me in trouble." She glanced down at her nakedness for the first time and used her trembling hands in a futile attempt to cover herself. "I guess he was right."

"Find anything good in here, sis?" Nathan asked from behind Amelia, startling her more than the apparition of the naked, weeping girl.

"Just her," Amelia said, pointing to the spot on the platform where she'd seen and spoken with Peg. Nathan had never acquired the ability to see the Life

Shadows, but Jenny had told them both it was a gift more common in females, and while Nathan had been curious, he'd accepted the fact he couldn't see them the way they could.

Nathan stepped up beside his sister to stare into the dark room. "Her who?" he asked. "Is there someone squatting in here? Ol' man Mathers was worried about that. If there is, I need to run them off before we start dismantling this thing, so no one gets hurt."

Amelia whipped her head around to find the dusty platform empty with no footprints in the dust or signs the girl had ever been there. "She's gone."

Her brother scanned the empty room. "There's only one way out and I sure didn't see anyone run by me."

Amelia ran a hand across her sweaty forehead. "I don't think she was alive, Bubba," she said uneasily, "and disappeared when you came in."

"Aww, shit, sis," Nathan said as he began to hum the X-Files theme and leaned back against the wall, "not more of that paranormal bullshit." He grabbed Amelia's shoulder and turned her to face him. "Don't you dare bring that up in front of Mom or she'll have your ass thrown in the nuthouse right along with Grandma Jen."

Amelia cocked a brow. "Yah, Elizabeth Ryan would certainly never win any daughter-of-the-year awards. Would she?"

"She did what she thought was right at the time," Nathan said in defense of his mother.

"She did it to look better to the snobs in Briarton, Nathan," Amelia said with a snort.

"And she'd do the same with you if you start

talking about seeing and talking to ghosts, sis. You know how she feels about that kinda bullshit."

"I have no doubt in the least," Amelia said with one last look at the empty platform. She rubbed at her aching temples. Encounters with the dead always brought on headaches. "Maybe I did just imagine it."

Nathan put his arm around his sister's shoulders to lead her from the room in the dark barn, and Amelia took comfort knowing her brother believed she'd seen the girl even if he couldn't. "Let me show you what I found on the other end. There's this great old porch swing I think I can take apart to use as a pattern."

Amelia smiled. "Porch swings sell great, Nathan. I have people asking for them all the time."

They stepped out into the sunshine and Amelia shielded her eyes against the glare. She rubbed at her temples. This headache was going to be a bad one, and Amelia wished she had some pain relievers in her purse.

2

———

THE BRIARTON PUBLIC LIBRARY HAD ALWAYS BEEN A special place of refuge for Amelia.

She'd spent hours there reading books about paranormal things she knew her mother wouldn't have approved of while she was in high school. Now she used the library's public computers to research property data and print it out.

Today Amelia wanted to see if anything had ever been recorded about the Mathers' barn out by Lake Hamilton. If that girl had died in the barn, there would surely be some record of it, even if it had been an accident. After an hour of fruitless searching, she hadn't come up with anything more than random stories about Lake Hamilton fishing tournaments and Fourth of July Celebrations from decades ago.

At a machine across from Amelia a young woman cursed in frustration again for the eighth or ninth time. Amelia got up to take a seat beside her. "You seem to be having as much trouble here today as I am. Is there something I could help you with? I'm Amelia Ryan."

With a suspicious glance, the young woman took Amelia's offered hand and shook it. "I'm Nancy Adams," she said, and I can't find shit on this damned thing today."

"Yah, me neither," Amelia said with a sympathetic sigh. "I'm looking for property records and old newspaper reports regarding some property but can't find shit." She smiled at the young woman. "What are you looking for?"

"I work for The Briarton Daily," she said, "and I'm supposed to be writing an obituary for Keith Hodges, but all I can find is fluff about him at Rotary Club Dinners or Chamber of Commerce Awards."

Amelia grinned. "The Hodges are old money in Briarton. Figure out his age and when he would have been in high school, then check the Briarton High yearbooks for those years. I'm sure you'll find plenty more fluff there and pictures from his glory days in team sports." Amelia began to gather her things. "If Keith was anything like his son Tommy, there'll be tons of pictures of him in the yearbooks."

"Thanks, Amelia," Nancy said, "I'd never have thought about that angle with a guy so old. He was like ninety and I wouldn't have thought they'd have had yearbooks back then."

"I know who he was. The family's owned Briarton Home Furnishings like forever, but he's not so old they only had slate and chalk in the schoolrooms." Amelia giggled.

"Since 1908," the girl said, doing a quick check of her notes on a yellow legal pad beside the computer. She did some scribbling. "I guess he'd have been in high school during or just after World War II."

Why are you doing your research here at the library and not over at the Daily?" Amelia asked.

Nancy took a deep breath. "Because I'm only a stringer and don't actually have a desk of my own at the office yet."

"And ol' man Kusak has you writing obituaries?"

The Kusak family had owned the Briarton Daily News since the turn of the century. Amelia had gone to school with members of the family, but like the Hodges, had never fit in with their circle. The Ryans were simple laborers not the business elite in Briarton and the O'Connors, of course, were crazy.

"He says I have to earn my stripes before I can have a seat at the table," Nancy said with a sad smile.

"Or a desk in the office?" Amelia added with a grin.

"I have a damned degree in Journalism from Northwestern," Nancy said with a shrug, "but I can't get that old sonofabitch to give me a shot."

Amelia smiled. "How long have you been in Briarton?"

"We moved here when I was a senior in high school," the young woman said. "My dad got a job working at the new prison as a guard."

Not only was this young woman a newcomer to Briarton, but her family came to town with the building of a prison the community hadn't really wanted in their midst. While it was good for the local economy, a prison in your back yard wasn't something socially acceptable and attracted a bad crowd. Amelia had seen it before and felt sorry for Nancy. She'd never fit in here the way she wanted to. Amelia wondered what had brought the young woman back to Briarton after attending a school like Northwestern.

"Want to grab some lunch, Nancy Drew?" Amelia asked with a grin. "Maybe I can give you some pointers to find your way around Briarton's close-knit society."

"Lunch sounds great," Nancy said with a grin at the Nancy Drew comment from Amelia, "but fuck Briarton's society. I just want to find a juicy story to shove under Kusak's nose he'll have to print with my name in the byline."

Amelia could only respect the young woman's spunk and enthusiasm. "I hope you find one soon, Nancy, but in the long run, Briarton is about as exciting as watching paint dry."

Nancy smiled. "What were you here in the library looking for today, Amelia?"

Did she dare tell this stranger her family secrets? Amelia decided to sidestep the issue of Life Shadows for the time being. They weren't something to discuss with a reporter looking for a story.

"My brother and I have a small business, tearing down old buildings, and recycling the wood and such into crafts we sell online and at Benson's Swap Meet."

"Barnwood Builders?" she asked with a broad smile on her pretty, freckled face. "I've seen the truck around town with the super-hot guy behind the wheel."

Amelia nodded and grinned. "My brother Nathan."

Nancy's smile widened. "Do you think he'd like a story done on him for the paper?" she asked. "Something like hometown boy goes big with old shit nobody else wants." She shrugged nervously and grinned. "You get my drift."

"I'm sure Nathan would accept any excuse to meet a pretty young woman like you. He's recently divorced and spends all his time working in the garage making furniture or with me, tearing down old buildings."

"And you were here today looking for research on one of those buildings?"

Amelia nodded. "An old barn out by Lake Hamilton. Do you know where that is?"

"My mother was on the committee to stop farmers from cutting off the streams and creeks that fed it with fresh water."

"Looks like she was unsuccessful."

"She's never given up," Nancy said with a shake of her head. "The house they bought was on the old banks of the lake and it's quite pitiful now that it's shrunk to nothing more than a mudhole."

"That never would have happened had the Briarton elite owned property there," Amelia said.

Nancy nodded. "By the time my parents bought their property at Lake Hamilton, the new Briarton Lake had been built and everybody who was anybody in Briarton had purchased property there." Nancy began typing. "I know that old barn," she said. "I used to walk my dog there." She seemed to shudder. "The place always creeped me out for some reason. I could never make myself go inside and Noodles, my Jack Russell terrier, would always throw a fit when we got close."

That made perfect sense to Amelia if Nancy was sensitive and had a little of the gift in her bloodline. Amelia knew dogs were sensitive to spirit energy and avoided places where the dead hung out.

"It is a creepy old barn," Amelia said without going

into too much detail. "Nathan says it's full of mice, bats, and snakes."

Nancy wrinkled her nose as she continued to type. "I'm glad I never ventured inside." She stopped typing and studied something on the screen. "Here's something that may be of interest."

"What?" Amelia asked and leaned in closer.

"This is from the Daily's archives they just computerized from microfiche," she said. "It's not exactly about that barn, but it's about a girl who went missing after a picnic at the lake back in 1947." Nancy turned to Amelia. "Is that the sort of stuff you were looking for?"

Amelia's eyes went wide when she saw the photograph of the pretty, dark-haired girl. She recognized the girl who called herself Peg. The name beneath the photograph said Margaret Adkins, aged fifteen. Missing after a school-sponsored picnic on May 7, 1947.

"That's exactly the sort of thing I was looking for. Can you print that for me?" Amelia asked.

"Sure." Nancy tapped a few buttons. "It'll print up at the librarian's desk and they'll charge you ten cents per page." Nancy studied the photograph. "Do you know who she was?"

Amelia shook her head. "No, but she's about the same age as my Grandma Jen. I want to take the article over to Rolling Acres nursing home and ask her about it."

"She's still in her right mind to answer questions like that?"

"Sharp as a tack," Amelia replied with a smile.

Nancy nodded and looked away. "My grandmother died in one of those horrid places. She thought she was six and kept crying for her mom and dad."

Amelia took the young woman's hand. "I'm so sorry, Nancy. That must have been horrible."

"It was worst on my mom," she said. "Grandma hadn't recognized her in years and died thinking she was her little sister and not her daughter."

"How terrible for her," Amelia said. She thought her mother should be ashamed to have thrown away so many years with a mother who loved her, in order to curry favor with families in Briarton who didn't give a shit about her.

Elizabeth had been an O'Connor and then a Ryan. She would always be working class of Irish ancestry and far beneath the recognition of any Kusak, Hodges, or Sizemore—no matter whose butt she tried to kiss.

Elizabeth had attempted to push Amelia into those cliques with Brownies, Girl Scouts, and 4-H, but Amelia had seen through it and paid little attention to the snobby girls who would never allow her into their little clubs or be her friends.

Elizabeth would chastise her when Amelia refused to attend birthday parties if she received an invitation or refused to send invitations to the snobs for her own parties. Her mother had gone so far as to cancel her birthday one year because she refused to hand-deliver invitations to the snooty girls she knew wouldn't attend anyhow.

Amelia had stormed at her mother that if taking invitations to those little bitches was so important to her then she should take them herself and had thrown the embossed, carefully addressed envelopes into her mother's face. Amelia had been ten, and that had been her last birthday party. To this day, the thought of her birthday turned Amelia's stomach.

———

A FEW DAYS after her meeting with Nancy at the library she sat down to supper with Nathan after a long day of sorting through online orders, packing boxes, and waiting at the UPS Store to ship the products.

Elizabeth was at the retro avocado-green stove, forking hamburgers onto a platter while her husband ripped open a bag of Lays Potato Chips to dump into a plastic serving bowl. Amelia had already opened a can of pork and beans and put them on the table with a jar of pickles, plastic squeeze bottles of mustard and ketchup, buns, and mayonnaise. Nathan had sliced tomatoes and onions. They were doing their Brady Bunch family dinner thing in the kitchen Elizabeth was so proud of with a green refrigerator to match the range and Formica countertops. Amelia found Mid-century Modern revolting and would rather have eaten outside on the patio or taken her plate to her room to eat at her desk in front of her flat-screen television, but Elizabeth insisted on the family eating together at least a few times a week.

She took the printed newspaper article and handed it to her brother. He read it then turned to Amelia in confusion. "What's this?"

"It's her," Amelia said. "It's the girl I saw in the barn."

Elizabeth heard the whispering and snatched the paper from Nathan's hand. "What's this?" she demanded, and Amelia was immediately put off by her mother's tone. "How could you possibly have seen a girl who went missing in 1947, Amelia?"

Amelia took a deep breath and forged ahead. "I

saw her Life Shadow, Mother. The poor thing was begging for help."

Elizabeth's face blanched and Amelia had difficulty controlling the grin tugging at the corners of her mouth. "Don't you dare bring that crazy talk into this house Amelia Ryan or I'll..."

Amelia furrowed her brow and glared up at her mother. "Or you'll what, Mother? Put me in an insane asylum like you did poor Grandma Jen?"

Elizabeth's blue eyes narrowed. "That crazy old bitch has poisoned your mind, Amelia, with her crazy talk of Life Shadows." She snorted a laugh. "Her fancy name for goddamned ghosts. Only crazy people think they can see and talk to ghosts, Amelia, and that's what your grandmother is—crazy."

Amelia pushed her chair back and stood to face her scowling mother. "Grandma sees them, Mother, and so do I." She pointed to the photograph in the newspaper article. "I saw that girl in the barn Nathan, and I visited. She was hurt, crying, and begging for help. Are you going to have me committed too? What sort of woman sends her own mother to an institution anyway?"

Amelia's smirk was knocked from her face by her mother's brutal slap. "I've done my best to erase the O'Connor legacy of insanity from this family, young lady, and I'll not have you digging it up again." Elizabeth grabbed Amelia by the shoulders and shook her. "If that's what you have in mind, Amelia, you can just get your freeloading ass out of my house this instant. Your father and I have already done our duty by you. We sent you to a good school, but you've wasted your education and slunk back home with your tail between your legs to make hobby art in your father's garage." Elizabeth grabbed one of Amelia's stenciled plaques from the wall and looked as though she intended to hit her daughter with it.

Nathan stood and took his mother by the wrist. "That's enough, Mom." Amelia could see deep sadness in her brother's eyes. "I had no idea you and Dad saw us as deadbeats and freeloaders, Mom."

Elizabeth's face softened as she studied her son's face. "Not you, Nate. You work hard every day making your beautiful furniture and you've been paying your father and I rent every month." Her eyes darted to her daughter. "Your sister just—"

"My sister just started this damned business, Mom, and keeps it running. If it weren't for her there wouldn't be anything to pay our rent with every month." When he saw Elizabeth's eyes go wide, he continued. "That's right, Mom, I said our rent. I worked out a price with Dad months ago for both my and Amelia's rooms and the use of the garage for the business."

"He did, Liz," Matthew Ryan mumbled as he put a burger on a bun. "I was sure I told you about it."

Amelia was sure he had as well, but Elizabeth had conveniently forgotten where the extra money was coming from every month.

"I ... I had no idea," Elizabeth stammered before grabbing the newspaper article from the table and wadding it in her fist, "but I'll not have this bullshit in my home, young lady. I've spent my whole adult life wiping the O'Connor insanity from the memory of Briarton." She pointed a trembling finger at Amelia with tears brimming in her eyes. "I'll not have another crazy bitch bringing it all back up again to tarnish the good Ryan name."

Amelia glared at her mother. "Don't worry, Mom, this crazy O'Connor bitch won't darken your damned door again." She turned and stormed toward her room with Nathan at her heels.

"I told you not to mention that shit in front of Mom, Amelia," he said in a harsh whisper. "You know how she is about it." Nathan watched his sister filling suitcases with her clothes, books, and shoes. "What the hell are you doing, sis?"

Amelia began stripping her bed. "This has been coming for a long time, Bubba. I have something lined up downtown," she gave her brother a quick peck on the cheek, "but I'm gonna have to hit up the company account for about three grand."

"Do we even have that much?" he asked with his eyes going wide.

Amelia grinned. "That much and a little more after yesterday's online deposits."

Nathan smiled and shrugged. "It's as much your business as mine, sis, but what are you renting—one of those condos on the lake?"

"Load up a couple of chairs, a headboard, a bookcase or two, and a few side tables," Amelia told him, "and I'll show you."

Amelia made a phone call and after Nathan loaded the furniture pieces onto the truck, he followed her to downtown Briarton, where she parked in front of an empty building on the west side of the Square.

The town had been established early in the nineteenth century with the original downtown built up around a central courthouse. Four main streets stretched out from the Square of central businesses.

In the early 1980s a Walmart came to Briarton and the businesses that made up the Square died. The buildings that once housed clothing stores, hardware stores, and pharmacies emptied to be replaced by junk and antique shops. Briarton now advertised itself as the antique capitol of the state. The Chamber of Commerce used that and Briarton Lake to attract tourists to the community. Wives could browse the antique malls while their husbands fished, and they could stay in one of the waterfront hotels.

Amelia parked her electric-blue Subaru Forester in front of a storefront that had once been a men's shoe store when Amelia was in high school but had stood empty for several years. Dust coated the inside of the two large windows facing the uneven sidewalk.

"What the hell is this, sis?" Nathan asked when he parked the pickup and got out.

She put a key into the lock and pushed open the door. "Welcome to the new home of Barnwood Builders, Incorporated."

Nathan stared around the empty space in awe. "Are you shittin' me?"

"We were gonna have to move it out of Dad's garage sooner or later," Amelia said with a grin. "There's an apartment upstairs I'm going to move into and a big garage off the back alley. I think this was originally a car dealership back in the Model-T days. We can move the workshop in there after I get the utilities turned on." Amelia smiled at her brother. "A guy I went to school with owns the building now, and he cut me a great deal on the rent since the business fits in so well with the antique malls around the Square.

"Let's have a look," Nathan said with a big grin on his face. He leaned against the wall and an old piece of paneling slipped off the studs to crash to the floor. "I can see we have a lot of work ahead of us, sis."

"It's better than living at Mom's," Amelia said with a deep sigh. "I'd offer to share the apartment, but it's only a one bedroom and you're too much of a slob for a futon in the living room." She grinned. "Could you build me a futon?"

Nathan stuck out his tongue. "I'm a slob?"

3

———

Nathan erected a sign made from the distressed barn wood Amelia had stenciled Barnwood Builders upon. It went up above the door and just below the apartment windows.

Amelia dressed the large store windows with red and white gingham curtains and set up tables displaying her crafts. Inside, she displayed Nathan's furniture and covered the freshly painted walls with her framed plaques and stenciled signs. The store had a homey feel and fit in well with the Briarton Antique Malls.

She met with a member of the Chamber of Commerce and purchased ad space in the promotional brochure they published through the Briarton Daily. Amelia also updated the Barnwood Builders website with a picture of the new storefront, business hours, and phone number.

They were planning the Grand Opening for the following weekend and Amelia had purchased ad space in several area papers to promote the event.

While Amelia set up a display one afternoon, Nancy strolled into the store. "This looks great,

Amelia," she said, staring around the space. "I bet you're going to do great here." She took the camera hanging around her neck and shot some photos. "Are you and that super-hot brother of yours ready to give me that interview for the Sunday Supplement?"

Nathan stepped in from the garage with a broad smile plastered across his face. "Super-hot brother is most definitely ready for an interview." He held his dust-covered hand out to Nancy. "Nathan Ryan," he said, "and who might you be?"

"Nancy Adams with the Briarton Daily News." Nancy took Nathan's hand with a smile and as soon as they touched, Amelia could see the spark between the two despite the twelve-year age difference. "We can do it now, if you'd like," the young woman said without releasing Nathan's hand.

Amelia studied her brother in his dusty work clothes. "Why don't we let my super-hot brother go home, take a shower, and change into some clean clothes first, Nancy? We can meet back here in my apartment and do the interview over drinks and dinner later this evening."

Nathan glanced down at the sawdust covering his clothes and blushed. "Sis is right. I should clean up first if I'm going to have drinks and dinner with a beautiful woman." He turned back toward the shop. "I have to put some braces on a piece I just glued up, then I'll go home, shower and change." Nathan grinned uneasily at Nancy. "Nice to meet you, Ms. Adams." He disappeared into the back and they heard a door close.

"Damn, he's hot," Nancy said with a grin on her pretty face. "And he's divorced?"

Amelia smiled. "Free as a bird as of last fall."

"Good to know," Nancy said with a sheepish grin. "Hey, I did a little more digging into that girl's disappearance—Margaret Adkins. She still has family here in Briarton—a sister named Grace Adkins Wells. She is a younger sister and is about eighty now."

"Good work, Nancy Drew. You have anything else?"

Amelia watched the woman's freckled cheeks flush. "I used a back door to get into the Sheriff's Office computer files and found a digital report."

"From 1947?" Amelia asked with her eyes going wide.

"Like the Daily, the Sheriff's Office has digitized their old files to make them easier to reference. They have copies of hand-written stuff in there going back before the turn of the century." Nancy grinned. "Real exciting stuff about old men being chased by dogs in the park and windows being broken by baseballs. Real riveting stuff. I should write some screenplays for CSI Briarton using some of it."

"I bet that would be a big hit." Amelia laughed. "And you know how to get into those files from any computer?"

Nancy grinned and picked up a small decorative box from a table. "You have your talents, Amelia, and I have mine."

"Just don't get caught. I'd hate to have to bail you out for hacking into the sheriff's office."

"They're all public records," Nancy said with a shrug of her narrow shoulders.

"So, what did you find in these public records?" Amelia asked.

"According to the police report, a kid named David

Sizemore was questioned about Margaret's disappearance."

Amelia snorted and gave a dismissive wave of her hand. "You don't have to say anymore. The damned investigation stopped right there."

"How'd you know?" Nancy asked with her blue eyes wide.

"Because if there was a royal family in Briarton, the Sizemores would be it. They opened the first bank in town before the turn of the century and while it folded with the Depression, the family still has its hooks in several businesses in town, including The Daily."

"Oh, my," Nancy said with a frustrated sigh. "I guess that means I shouldn't use this investigative piece as my big story to put in front of Kusak to earn my stripes."

"The truth is still the truth, Nancy, and if The Daily won't print it, I bet there are other papers in the area that would jump at it." Amelia grinned. "The Sizemore reach doesn't stretch much past Briarton."

Nancy smiled and ran a hand through her shoulder-length strawberry-blonde hair. "I want to go get some more shots of that barn before your brother and his crew have it torn down. You wanna tag along?"

The official opening wasn't for a few more days and Amelia could use the fresh air. "Sure, why not."

"Wow," Nancy exclaimed as she parked her Toyota in front of the old barn, "they've really come a long way with this."

Not much of the old structure remained. The timbers leaned some and Nathan's crew had supports screwed to all four corners to prop it up. Amelia got out of Nancy's car and walked toward the end of the barn where she'd seen Peg's weeping apparition. She wondered if the girl would still be there after all the noise of the deconstruction.

As she neared the opening, Amelia heard the weeping and sobbing of the young girl again. Peg was still there.

Nancy followed a few paces behind Amelia, shaking her head. "Damn, this place still creeps me the fuck out."

Amelia cocked a brow and stopped Nancy's progress. "Do you hear anything?" She nodded toward the barn. "Anything at all?"

Nancy turned her head toward the barn and her face screwed up in confusion. "A girl crying maybe," she mumbled with her eyes moving to the swaying treetops. "Probably just the wind in the trees, though. Right?" she asked with one brow cocked.

Amelia led Nancy into the room. Most of the wall boards had been pried away. The only structure visible was the raised floor the apparition of Peg knelt upon. "What do you see?" Amelia asked the young reporter and nodded toward the platform.

"Blue light coming in through the bushes," Nancy said with a shiver in her voice as she squeezed Amelia's hand. "What do you see and hear?"

Amelia trusted this young woman. She wasn't sure why, but she did. Maybe it was time to share the family secret.

"I see Peg, and she's crying," Amelia admitted.

"Really?" the young woman gasped. "Like a ghost or something?"

Amelia nodded. "My grandmother calls them Life Shadows."

"Life Shadows is cool," Nancy said, considering

the title. "Can you talk to Life Shadows?"

"Sometimes."

Nancy's face turned from one of fright to excitement. "Let's interview her then and ask what happened to her. Why is she still here?"

"Peg?" Amelia said in a soft, even voice. "May I ask you some questions?"

Peg turned her tear-streaked face to stare at them. "Your friend wants to know what they did to me," she said, and her swollen eyes narrowed in anger. "I'll show her what they did to me," the girl's apparition said in a tone that sent a chill down Amelia's spine.

Nancy's face went pale before she was shoved to her knees and yelped in surprise. Amelia could see the ghostly figures of two young men, but they weren't as clear as Peg's form that had superimposed itself over Nancy on the barn floor. The young men laughed as they tore Peg's clothes off and tossed them aside. They called her filthy names, slapped, and pinched her. Nancy/Peg screamed in pain as the apparition behind her laughed and shoved his erection between her naked ass cheeks and pumped with vigor. The one in front assaulted the girl's mouth as he cackled with his friend. "Make the bitch swallow it all," the one in behind said. "I'll shove home from this end, and we can meet in the middle."

"Stop it," Amelia screamed as she watched her new friend writhing in the dirt, but it didn't stop. Nancy and Peg continued to be brutalized by the two young men while Amelia stood watching helpless to do anything.

"You have to see it all to understand," Peg whispered in an ethereal voice only Amelia could hear.

As the boy behind Peg told the boy in front to

shove it home, Nancy choked and gagged. Then the boy behind slid his belt from his pants and wrapped it around Peg's throat. He pulled it tight in his strong hands and rode her in a grotesque parody of a rodeo rider on a bucking bronc.

"My daddy says this is the best way to experience a trashy piece of filth like this. "Ride her like a horse until she drops," the boy behind said as he cackled.

Both boys laughed as they drove their penises home with their groaning releases.

"She's not moving," the boy standing above Peg's head said as he knelt. "I think she's dead." He shot to his feet and stared at the other young man. "What are we gonna do?"

"Go back to the picnic and get fucking drunk," the laughing boy said. "She's trash. Nobody's gonna miss the likes of her." He kicked Peg's naked torso as he zipped his trousers. "She had a nice tight asshole though. How was her mouth?"

The other boy looked up from Peg's body and grinned. "Nice. She took the whole damned thing down her throat. I think I shot my wad directly into her damned belly."

They began to walk away. "My dad takes me to a whore in West Town who can swallow a cock like that," the boy from behind said. "Quite a feeling, isn't it?"

When they disappeared, the apparition of Peg lay naked and silent in the dirt. Nancy gasped and panted. "What the hell just happened to me?" she coughed with a look of horror on her pale, freckled face.

Amelia rushed to Nancy's side. "Those bastards raped and killed that poor girl in here," Nancy gasped as she crawled to her knees. "Did you see it?" she asked Amelia as if trying to reconcile what she'd just experienced. "One of them choked her with his penis while the other one choked her with his belt," Nancy gasped as she massaged her throat, "and I could feel it all. I felt her fucking die, Amelia." Tears welled in the young woman's eyes and Amelia wanted to pull her into her arms and hold her like the little sister she'd never had.

"Peg wanted both of us to see what they did to her," Amelia said. "I think she needed to do that in order to move on."

"I don't think she's gone," Nancy said, looking past Amelia to the wooden platform where Peg knelt violently weeping. "She's still there and crying."

"Please take me home now," the girl begged. "I want to go home to my mama. She must be worried sick, and Daddy is probably mad as hell at her for letting me go on the picnic." The blue apparition tried to step from the platform but couldn't. An invisible force stopped her, and she wailed in frustration. "Please take me to my mama or go tell her where I am so she can come get me." Peg fell to her bare knees and wept. "I just want to go home."

Amelia's heart ached for the poor girl as the hair on her arms stood erect. "Who were those boys, Peg? Who did that to you?"

Peg's apparition began to fade. "I can't tell," she wept. "They'll hurt my little sister, Gracie, if I tell." Peg vanished, and the space grew still except for the breeze in the trees, the croaking of bullfrogs, and the quacking of ducks on what was left of nearby Lake Hamilton.

Nancy sat with her back against a post. "What the hell just happened to me, Amelia?" she asked, dashing tears from her face. "I'd swear two boys just beat, raped, and strangled me to death."

"It's what they did to Margaret Adkins." Amelia helped the trembling young woman to her feet.

"Did you know your Life Shadows could do that?"

Amelia shook her head. "I'm gonna have to have a long talk with my Grandma Jen about a few things."

"We should probably have a talk with Margaret's sister too," Nancy said as they exited the barn. "Maybe she'll have some idea who those bastards were."

"You know who she is?"

Nancy nodded. "Grace Adkins Wells. She and her brother Thomas live in that big old brick house next to the library on West Main."

"Well, dust yourself off, Nancy Drew and let's go have a chat with sister Grace to see if we can put a story together for you to print in the Briarton Daily."

"It would read more like a horror novel than a newspaper story," Nancy said as they returned to her Camry.

"Write a novel, then."

"I want to be a journalist not a novelist," Nancy protested.

Amelia snorted. "With some of the Fake News I read online these days, you could do either and still be a writer."

"I've always been more about fact than fiction," the young reporter said.

"The facts I've lived with most of my life would read like fucking fiction," Amelia said. "Would you have believed what just happened in there if it hadn't happened to you?"

Nancy ran a trembling hand through her strawberry-blonde hair. "I'm still not sure I believe it."

4

Grace Adkins Wells was a sweet woman in her late seventies or early eighties.

"May I help you?" the stooped, white-headed woman wearing a pink sweat suit asked when she opened the door to Amelia and Nancy.

Nancy extended her hand. "I'm Nancy Adams with The Briarton Daily News," she said, "and this is Amelia Ryan."

"Amelia O'Connor actually," Amelia corrected and gave Nancy an 'I'll explain later' glance.

"We're here," Nancy continued, "because the paper is doing some updates on old stories printed in the Daily and one of those stories had to do with the disappearance of your sister Margaret in 1947."

The old woman's face drained of color and she clutched at the door for support. "Poor Peg's been gone for a very long time now, young woman," the old woman mumbled. "What do you hope to accomplish by bringing it all back up at this point?"

"Do you have any idea what happened to your sister, Miss Adkins?" Amelia asked. "I'd really like to get your side of things."

"Won't you come in?" Grace asked. "This isn't a discussion to hold in the open doorway."

Amelia and Nancy followed the woman into a comfortably appointed living room with furnishings that probably were new when Nixon lived in the White House. An old man snored in a brown leather recliner. "My brother Thomas," Grace said. "He was a year older than Peg and I was five years younger." With a nod, she offered them a seat on the beige velvet couch covered in clear plastic but didn't bother to wake her brother.

"What do you think happened to your sister, Grace?" Nancy asked as the reporter.

Grace glanced at her sleeping brother. "I don't really know," she said with a touch of sadness in her voice. "My Aunt Eunice swore Peg ran away because Daddy was so hard on her, but I never believed that."

"Why?" Nancy persisted.

"Why would she run away or why didn't I believe it?" the old woman offered.

"Both, if you please," Nancy said. "I'd like to have a clear picture of the family dynamic."

The old woman took a deep breath. "Our father was raised in a very strict and religious household," Grace said, "which he used as a model for ours. The boys got jobs as soon as they could wield a rake and the girls were kept close to home and away from boys. We weren't allowed to socialize with boys outside church activities and family functions. Our marriages were arranged by the adults." She sighed. "I never laid eyes on my husband until I walked down the aisle and saw him standing there."

"That must have made for an uncomfortable wedding night," Amelia muttered.

The old woman shrugged her pink-clad shoulders. "It's the way things were done then and made for fewer unwed mothers."

"But Margaret attended the picnic at Lake Hamilton with her school friends," Amelia said.

Grace rolled her old eyes. "Daddy had forbidden her going, but Mama let her sneak off that day. Mama had a soft spot for Peggy and wanted her to have more of a life than Daddy would allow."

Thomas Adkins coughed and roused up in the recliner. "And she paid for it good when Peggy didn't come home that night, now didn't she, Gracie?"

"Our Daddy was a stern man," Grace said. "He was considered hard even for those times and would be called abusive now by the politically correct crowd."

"He beat your mother?" Nancy asked with a raised brow.

"That hardass sonofabitch beat all of us," Thomas said and coughed to clear his throat again. "Had Peggy come home that night, he'd have beaten her and Mama both black and blue with his damned belt." He coughed harder and Grace got up, saying she was going to the kitchen for some water and her brother's medication.

"What do you think happened to your sister, Mr. Adkins?" Nancy asked when the man grew quiet.

"I've had my suspicions over the years," the old man mumbled into his sleeve.

"What suspicions?" Amelia asked.

"I suppose you know about her diary."

Nancy nodded. "The original newspaper article mentioned the police had taken it and that they'd questioned David Sizemore because Margaret had mentioned him in it."

"Sizemore's not the only one the police should have dragged in for questioning," the old man spat.

"Who else?" Nancy asked in a gentle, prodding tone.

Amelia smiled as she watched the young reporter at work. *Kusak's a fool for not giving this gal a shot. She certainly knows her stuff when it comes to questioning someone.*

"That drunken fool Hodges," the old man said.

"Keith Hodges?" Nancy asked. "He just died." She'd just written the man's obituary article for The Daily.

The old man had another coughing fit, and Grace rushed to her brother's side, offering a tall glass of iced water with slices of lemon floating in it and a handful of pills. He took them from her and swallowed.

"They all said Keith came back from Korea a drunk because of what he saw over there," Grace said. "Lots of those boys did."

"That asshole came home a drunk because of something that happened right here before he ever enlisted," her brother sneered. "His old man made him enlist, hoping it would straighten his ass out, but it was already too late for that."

"And you think that something had to do with the disappearance of your sister, Mr. Adkins?" Amelia asked.

"Thomas has always thought David Sizemore and Keith Hodges had something to do with Peggy's disappearance," Grace said as she stared at her brother who was nodding off again.

"Do you have any pictures of your sister I might use in my article?" Nancy asked in a whisper as the old man began to snore.

"I have the '47 Briarton High Yearbook," she said. "There are pictures of everyone involved in it. Would that do?"

"That would be fabulous," Nancy said. "Thank you."

The old woman left the room. "What do you think?" Amelia asked her new friend.

"I think there is a shitload of circumstantial evidence here," Nancy said with a sigh. "Too bad that Hodges motherfucker is already in the ground."

"What about Sizemore?" Amelia whispered. "Where is he?"

"In a home somewhere," the young reporter said. "I guess he had some bad heart attacks and the family didn't want him living alone anymore."

"I'll leave figuring out where that is to you, Nancy Drew," Amelia said with a good-natured giggle.

Nancy grinned. "I want to find him and interview him as soon as possible."

"Before he's taking a dirt nap too?" Amelia said with a cocked brow.

"Exactly." Nancy nodded. "Not all of us can have conversations with the already departed like you."

"Here's that yearbook," Grace said as she hurried into the room carrying a red yearbook with the old Briarton High building embossed on the cover.

A new building had been erected when Amelia was a Freshman and the old one, built at the turn of the century, torn down. The two women flipped through the glossy pages until they found the class photos. Margaret's was at the beginning of the Junior year pages and Amelia recognized it as the same photo used in the newspaper article about her disappearance. The girl had been pretty with big brown eyes set into a heart-shaped face framed by long brown hair styled for the post-war period.

"She was a very pretty girl," Amelia said.

Grace smiled. "Peg worked on her hair for hours to get those bangs to curl like that. She wanted to look like a movie star for that picture."

"She was certainly pretty enough," Nancy said. "Was she involved in theatre?"

"She tried out for some school plays," Grace told them with a sad smile, "but you know how it was."

Amelia nodded. "Her name wasn't Kusak or Hodges, or she wasn't dating someone with the right name, so she didn't get a part."

Grace snorted. "Just a walk on as a maid in something or other as I recall."

"Then she must have actually been pretty good," Amelia said with a sigh. "I never even got that." She glanced at Nancy. "Ryan and especially O'Connor were not names to get you parts in plays or musicals at Briarton High."

Nancy grinned. "Somehow I don't see you dressed up like an Austrian schoolgirl belting out "The Sound of Music"."

"Oklahoma actually," Amelia said with a nervous chuckle.

"What is it?" she snapped when Amelia saw the color drain from Nancy's face.

She saw a picture of two smiling boys tossing a beachball to one another. The caption read: Fun in the sun at the Briarton High spring picnic. Keith Hodges and David Sizemore having a ball. The boys wore white dress shirts and pleated trousers. Clothes Amelia would have considered a bit too formal for a picnic, but what boys like Sizemore and Hodges might have worn to uphold their social standing at the time.

"It's them," Nancy muttered through trembling lips. "I'll never forget those faces for as long as I live." Tears brimmed in the young woman's eyes. "Or what they did with their nasty little dicks."

Amelia had to remember that Nancy had just experienced what had happened to Margaret as if it were happening to her. She'd been savagely raped and murdered. Amelia didn't know what sort of scar that experience was going to leave on the young woman, and a pang of guilt stabbed at her heart for putting Nancy in that situation.

"Is everything all right?" Grace asked in a soft voice.

Nancy blinked back her tears and smiled at the old woman. "Would you mind if I borrowed this to copy some of the photos for my article?"

"You can keep it," Grace said. "The memories in that damned book are too painful. I haven't opened it in decades."

"Are you sure?" Nancy clutched the book in her petite hands. "Because I can run it back over here to you after I've made the copies I want."

Thomas began to cough again. "We should be on our way, Miss Adkins," Amelia said as she urged Nancy to her feet. "Thank you so much for your time." She patted the yearbook. "This will do so much to improve my article."

"Oh, no," the old woman said as she settled her brother in the recliner, "thank you girls for looking into poor Peggy's disappearance again. Nobody gave a lick about it or her back then. They said she ran away because Daddy was to strict, but I knew that wasn't true. Peggy would never have just run off without telling me she planned to do it." Tears ran down her wrinkled face. "And if she had run off, she'd have let me know where she'd landed after a while. It's been seventy years. Sisters just don't do that."

Nancy patted the old woman's pale, age-spotted hand. "Of course they don't, and we'll do our best for your poor sister."

Grace led them out. The late afternoon sun shone through the tall maples in the Adkins yard, and the shadows of the fluttering leaves dappled the concrete sidewalk along West Main Street.

Nancy clutched the old yearbook to her chest. "We've got to find this Sizemore bastard and make him pay for what he did to that poor girl, Amelia." She took out her phone. "I need to call the office and talk to Kusak. I think we might have a hell of a story here, and I want to get his OK to go ahead with it."

"I know, sweetheart," Amelia said with a sigh, "but knowing what they did and proving it are two very different things when the case is seventy years old; we have no body, and the suspects are from Briarton's elite." Nancy walked off with the phone at her ear. Amelia waited in the shade, enjoying the Spring breeze with the aroma of lilacs heavy from nearby shrubs.

Nancy rubbed at her throat as she returned and stuffed her phone into her pocket. "I can still feel whatever it was he wrapped around my neck while he was ..." Nancy brushed a hand over her backside. "Nobody's ever done that to me before, Amelia," she said with a sob, "and nobody's ever going to do it to me again."

"Are you going to be all right to interview me and

Nathan this evening?" Amelia asked. "We can do it another day if you need a break."

Nancy ran a hand through her hair. "No, I'm all right. Kusak wants this interview for a Sunday Supplement and I'm sure as hell not going to mess up my chance at a byline."

When they parked in front of the store, Nancy pointed to the new sign. "What's up with that? Proprietor Amelia O'Connor? I thought your name was Ryan."

Amelia shrugged. "It's a family thing. O'Connor is my grandmother's name—the grandmother I inherited my little gift from and my red hair."

They went inside, and Amelia ordered pizzas and salads from Domino's. She texted Nathan and asked him to bring beer when he was ready.

When he arrived, Nathan handed Amelia the twelve-pack of Budweiser with a grim look on his face. "Mom saw the sign today and there's gonna be hell to pay, sis."

"She's the one who said I was acting more like a crazy O'Connor than a Ryan," Amelia said with a shrug. "As if the Ryans are the sane ones in this damned family."

Nathan grinned. "Is that pizza I smell?"

Amelia winked at Nancy and grinned. "Nose like an Irish Setter on this one, I tell ya."

————

THE PHONE RANG at Briarton Home Furnishings. Thomas Hodges glanced around for his secretary, but she wasn't at her desk. He frowned when he saw the clock and picked up the receiver. Who would be calling the store after hours?

"Briarton Home Furnishings. This is Tom. How may I help you?"

"Tom, this is Bob Kusak at the paper, and I think you might have a problem."

"If it's something with the advertising package," Tom said, irritated at the man for calling so late, "you'll have to call back during business hours to talk to Connie. She handles all that."

"This has nothing to do with business, Tom. It's a personal matter having to do with your father."

"Dad's been dead for almost a month, Bob. What kind of trouble could he possibly be in now?"

He heard the man take a deep breath on the other end of the phone. "I have a new reporter here who's trying to earn her stripes and she's dug up an old story that seems to involve your dad and David Sizemore during their days back at Briarton High."

Tom chuckled. "That would be ancient fucking history then."

"It has to do with a girl who went missing from their class and is now presumed dead." Kusak took another deep breath. "Did your dad ever mention a Peggy or Margaret Adkins?"

Tom squeezed his eyes shut as the memory of his father, drunk again, and huddled on the garage floor, rocking back and forth with an old yearbook in his hands as he begged someone named Peggy to forgive them. He'd gone to his father and asked him what was wrong, but all the man would say through his drunken tears was that you could kill a girl by putting your dick down her throat.

Tom had brushed it off as more of his father's drunken ramblings, but now he didn't know.

"Tom?" Kusak said. "Did your father ever mention the girl in connection with David Sizemore?"

"He and David were best friends," Tom said, floundering for an answer to the newspaper man's question, "but I don't think he ever mentioned a girl by that name. Have you talked to David?"

"His will be my next call. I just wanted you to know what's going on here."

"Does this reporter intend to drag my poor dad's name through the mud over this?"

"It's still all just speculation at this point, Tom, and I'll try to keep her reined in. The paper did a story on the girl's disappearance back in '47 and this reporter is just rehashing it. I don't even think your dad was mentioned in the original story, but Sizemore was. Your dad probably won't come up in connection with it this time either."

"Let's try to keep it that way, Bob. Briarton Home Furnishings does a lot of business with The Daily and I'd hate to see that change over some ancient foolishness."

"Sure thing, Tom. Thanks for your time."

Amelia visited her grandmother at Rolling Acres on Sundays.

She arrived to find Jennifer O'Connor in good spirits with her bright red hair freshly styled in the fashion of Miss Kitty from Gun Smoke.

"I see you and your brother made the paper today," her grandmother said with a grin. "Or is he not your brother any longer? I see they say your name is Amelia O'Connor now and not Amelia Ryan."

Amelia grinned as she handed her grandmother a Starbuck's Frappe. "Mom and I had a big fight and she threw me out of the family—again."

Jennifer took her granddaughter's hand. "Have you been seeing Life Shadows again?"

"And made the mistake of mentioning it in front of Mom," Amelia said with a nod.

"I fear your mother is simply jealous because she was never blessed with our gift, Amelia."

"She calls it a curse and not a gift, Grandma and she doesn't want any reminders of that curse in her damned house."

The ungifted sometimes see themselves as

cursed," Jennifer said as she sipped the Starbucks Frappe Amelia had brought her. "Tell me about what you saw, child."

Amelia shook her head at the memory. "It was pretty awful, Grandma." She swallowed some of her own Frappe, enjoying the cold, sweet coffee shake running down her throat. "Did you know a girl named Margaret Adkins when you were in school?"

Jennifer sipped through the straw while she searched her memories. "Peggy Adkins?"

"That's the one," Amelia said. "I thought she'd have been about your age."

"She was a year behind your grandfather and I, but I knew her. She was in my Biology class and really smart. Girls weren't supposed to do well in science, but Peggy got straight As and it really pissed off some of the boys in class because Mr. Hankins graded on a curve." Jennifer set the tall Venti cup on her bedside table and picked up a biscotti. "Was it her Shadow you saw?" Jennifer bit into the cookie and chewed.

"In an old barn out by what's left of Lake Hamilton," Amelia said with a nod. "Nathan is tearing down the barn and I went out there with him to check it out."

"And Peggy is there?" Jennifer asked and picked up her cup. "As I recall, she went missing after the Spring Picnic our Senior year." She stared off into the room. "It would have been in '47 I think.

"Were you there at the picnic?"

Jennifer smiled. "No, your grandfather couldn't go because he had to help his father with the planting." She sipped more of the icy coffee drink. "I wouldn't go without him." She grinned at her granddaughter. "That wasn't done back then. When you were going with a boy, you didn't attend functions without him." Jennifer picked up the biscotti. "I don't think Peggy had a boyfriend at the time. After she disappeared, the paper said the police found her diary and it mentioned David Sizemore, as I recall."

"Did you know him?"

"Everyone knew David Sizemore and his shadow Keith Hodges. They were the two heart-throbs of Briarton High in my day, but I had your grandfather, so they were of no interest to me," Jenny said with a sigh, "but they were nothing but trouble."

"Trouble?" Amelia asked between bites of her biscotti and sips of her Frappe. "What sort of trouble?"

"You know," Jennifer said with her pale cheeks turning pink, "putting their hands on girls where they shouldn't have been putting them and making lewd comments in the hallways about it."

"Things I'm sure they never got in trouble for at Briarton High because of their names," Amelia hissed.

"Those two could have gotten away with murder in Briarton."

"I think they did, Grandma," Amelia said.

Jennifer's head jerked up to stare at her granddaughter. "What did you see, child? Tell me."

Amelia went on to explain her initial encounter with the Life Shadow of Peggy Adkins and her plea to be taken home. Then she told her grandmother about what had happened when she'd taken poor Nancy to the barn.

"Those poor girls," Jennifer said, shaking her head. "Peggy is dead, and your friend now bears the psychological scars of a rape victim."

"I didn't know that could happen, Grandma. I feel terrible for Nancy."

"Your young friend is blessed with the gift to some degree or it wouldn't have," Jennifer said. "Peggy is frightened and angry about what happened to her. She wanted you to know what happened to her and showing you in that fashion was the only way she knew how." Jennifer shook her coifed red head. "I wish I'd known or had thought to look for her there back when it happened."

"You couldn't have known, Grandma. Don't blame yourself for things out of your control." Amelia took her grandmother's hand. "The ones to blame are David Sizemore and Keith Hodges. They're the ones who raped and murdered Peggy Adkins in that barn."

"Keith is dead now," Jennifer said, "I saw it in the paper. Said he died peacefully in his bed with his loving family in attendance." She snorted. "He was a drunken wreck of a man who died in terrible pain from a rotted liver."

Amelia raised her brow. "How do you know that, Grandma?"

Jennifer chuckled. "The geriatric grapevine." She sucked the last of her Frappe from the cup with a loud sputtering sound. You wouldn't believe the gossip in this damned place."

"Better than at the asylum?"

"The gossip there was much more entertaining," Jennifer said with a grin, "but difficult to sort out sometimes. I know most everyone here and their histories." Amelia watched her grandmother's face turn grim. "He's here, you know."

Amelia jerked her head up to stare around the room. "Who's here?"

"Not in my room, child. Here in Rolling Acres. David Sizemore lives here in the home." Jennifer leaned her neatly coifed red head in toward Amelia. "His family has him in one of those expensive assisted living suites up on the top floor, but he comes down to watch television with us peasants sometimes."

"How special for you." Amelia grinned at her grandmother's smile.

"He's still the same stuck-up bastard he was in school and I wouldn't give him the time of day or piss on him if his fancy silk pajamas were on fire." Jennifer reached out for her granddaughter. "Do you think we could go visit your grandfather?" Jennifer swiped a tear from her cheek. "It's been such a very long time since I saw his handsome face."

Amelia raised a brow. "Then you want to go to Prairie Road and not the cemetery."

"You know he's not at the damned cemetery, child."

Ned O'Connor had been killed in an automobile accident on Prairie Road east of Briarton in 1975 and that was where his Life Shadow remained. Elizabeth had her mother committed because the woman insisted on going to the spot her husband died to visit with him. People in town talked, and Jennifer ended up in Lockwood Asylum.

That facility had been shut down during the Reagan administration and Jennifer had been returned by bus without warning to Briarton. Elizabeth had immediately had her mother confined in the newly opened Rolling Acres with strict orders to the management that she not be allowed out without Elizabeth's express consent. Amelia and Nathan had both attempted to spring their grandmother for a day out to visit their grandfather but had been thwarted by the vigilant staff.

"You know I can't Grandma, but I'll stop by Prairie Road and tell Grandpa you're doing all right."

"I'd appreciate that, Amelia." Jennifer took a deep breath. "If you and your friend saw Peggy in that barn, it's where she died, and her Life Shadow is stuck there for some reason. Did they find her body there?"

Amelia shook her head. "Margaret Adkins' body has never been found."

"You say your brother and his crew are tearing the barn down?"

"There's not much of it left," Amelia said as she cleaned up the Starbucks cups and bags.

Jennifer grabbed her granddaughter's wrist. "She's got to be there someplace, Amelia. You and Nathan have to find her and return her to her family, or she'll never be free of that place."

Amelia bent and kissed her grandmother's forehead. "We will, Grandma, but I bet that bastard Sizemore knows exactly where she is. He had to have been the one who hid her body after they killed her."

Jennifer grinned. "Maybe I'll ask him the next time he struts into the television room in his fancy silk pajamas and robe."

Amelia's mouth fell open. "Don't you dare provoke that sonofabitch, Grandma. He's a killer and I think he enjoyed it."

"Don't worry, sweetheart," Jennifer said, "I'm not quite as crazy as your mother thinks I am and I doubt the old bastard has the balls to do anything without his counterpart, Hodges at his side. As a matter of fact, Hodges was probably the one who Sizemore had hide the body. I don't see that smarmy bastard getting his hands dirty with something like manual labor."

Amelia smiled and kissed her grandmother again.

"I know you're not crazy, Grandma, but stay away from Sizemore. He's dangerous and could be unpredictable."

"Tell your grandfather about Peggy," Jennifer said. "He was fond of her and spent weeks with the search party looking for her. He'll be happy to know you found her after all this time."

Amelia kissed her grandmother again. "I will, Grandma."

Amelia got in her Subaru and drove out of town toward Prairie Road. She stopped in the spot Ned O'-Connor had lost his life, but Amelia didn't see him. Did the dead have social lives? Was her grandfather out having beers with his dead friends?

Amelia called his name a few times, but when he didn't appear, she got back into her car and returned to the store and her apartment.

She'd used her Home Depot credit card and pur-chased new stainless steel appliances for the kitchen, updated the cabinets, and covered the floors in plank vinyl flooring. Nathan had changed out the fixtures in the bathroom for new ones, and she'd supplemented the pieces of his furniture with new pieces. A new pil-low-top mattress was on her bed and billowy sheers hung at the tall windows. The apartment was comfort-able and done to her tastes—not her mother's and not her former husband's. She preferred shabby chic to modern and the apartment reflected laid back comfort rather than cold sophistication. She had worn paper-backs on her bookshelves and drank her boxed wine from odd-colored wine glasses.

Amelia could honestly say she was in a happy place in her life for the first time in a very long time and she hoped very much to stay there.

Tom Hodges knocked on the door of the second-floor room at Rolling Acres. A woman in blue scrubs answered the door. "May I help you?"

"I'm Tom Hodges and I'm here to see David Sizemore."

"Mr. David is having his supper now, sir," the woman said.

"Who is it, Mamie?" a male voice called from inside the apartment.

"It's a Mr. Hodges here to see you, sir."

"Keith?" the man called as cigarette smoke billowed out the door. "Let him in, you old fool woman, let him in."

Mamie opened the door and let Tom inside the apartment. David Sizemore wore pajamas as he sat in a wheelchair at a round kitchen table with a cigarette between two fingers. "It's not dad, Uncle David," Tom said as he stepped inside. "It's Tom—Tom Hodges."

The balding old man put his cigarette out in the mashed potatoes on his plate and smiled up at Tom. "Tom, of course," the old man said and coughed. "Come on in." He pushed his plate aside. "I'd offer you something to eat but you wouldn't want any of this swill." The woman grabbed the plate before he pushed it off the table. "Where's your dad, boy. I haven't seen him in months."

"Dad passed away last month, Uncle David," Tom said as he took a seat in a rolling chair at the dinette. "You were at the funeral with Lilly and Ray."

David's watery, blue eyes darted around the room in confusion. "I was?" he mused. "A funeral?"

"Your daughter and son-in-law took you Mr.

David," the nursing assistant said, "and then you went out to eat at Red Robin after the graveside service. Remember?"

The old man grinned. "Red Robin," he sang the commercial jingle, "yumm!"

"If you're going to be here to sit with Mr. David for a bit," the woman said, "I'm gonna go have my supper in the nurse's lounge."

"I'll be here for a while," he said. "Take your time."

The woman left, and David Sizemore's demeanor changed completely. His hands stopped trembling, he took a cigarette from the pack on the table, and he straightened in the wheelchair. "I didn't think that nosey old bitch would ever leave." He lit the cigarette and inhaled. "What can I do for you, Tom?"

"I got a call from Bob Kusak at the paper," he said. "Did he call you?"

David shook his head. "That old bitch screens all my calls for Lilly. I wouldn't know if he called or not." He took another puff on the cigarette. "What's this all about, Tom?"

"Bob says he has a reporter looking into the disappearance of a girl back when you and dad were in high school—a girl named Peggy."

Tom watched the old man's eyes go wide. He waited for him to say something, but he never did. "Does that name mean anything to you, Uncle David? I think it would have to my dad."

"Your dad was too sensitive." He dropped the cigarette on the floor and crushed it out on the carpet.

"What's that supposed to mean? Did you and my dad know that girl?"

David smiled. "Everybody knew Leggy Peggy," he said with a cackling laugh. "That little bitch would lay down and spread her legs for anybody with a hard dick."

"You and my dad screwed her?"

David laughed. "She gave your dad a good damned suck once. A suck Keith never forgot."

"In that barn out by Lake Hamilton?"

The old man's eyes went wide again. "Who said anything about that barn?"

"It's where that reporter says the two of you took her and that's where they're looking for her remains."

"Well, they won't find her in no damned barn. She spread her legs for some stranger passing through and ran off with him to Chicago or St. Louis or someplace far away from Briarton." He lit another cigarette. "Her old man was a woman beater and was probably screwing Peggy and her sister too. Low-life men like that do that sorta thing you know."

"Is that what you told the police back then?" Tom asked.

He shrugged. "I told the police the truth back then and they never brought it up to me again."

Tom nodded and stood. "All right, Uncle David. Do you want me to stay here with you until your nurse comes back?"

"No," he said, getting to his feet and reaching for his robe on the hat rack. "I think I'll go down to the lounge and watch a little television with the pretty ladies of Rolling Acres."

"You don't want me to push you down in your chair?" Tom asked as he watched the old man shuffle across the room in his leather slippers.

Sizemore snorted. "That contraption is just for looks," he said with a wink. "This old dog can still get around just fine."

Tom studied the old man with a frown on his face. David Sizemore was out to protect David Sizemore, and he had no doubt that if push came to shove, the old bastard would throw his dad under the bus in this situation with the girl.

6

———

ON MONDAY MORNING, AMELIA AND NANCY DROVE OUT to the barn to see the progress.

"It's sure a pretty day," Nancy said as she stared up at the bright, blue sky.

"It must have been a day just like this when Sizemore and Hodges killed that poor girl," Amelia said as she turned down the gravel road leading to the barn.

Nancy flipped through her notepad and sighed. "Almost to the day seventy years ago."

"What the hell?" Amelia gasped when they neared the barn to see a bulldozer belching black smoke as it backed off a trailer.

She parked her Subaru and she and Nancy jumped out. Amelia ran to where her brother stood talking to two men beside the leaning skeletal remains of the old barn.

"What's going on here, Nathan? What's with the damned dozer?"

"Mr. Mathers and his son think we should doze the remains of the structure before it falls down and someone gets hurt," Nathan explained as he ran a hand through his thick curls.

Amelia turned to the men gathered around Nathan. "We think there's a very good chance that a dead body is hidden in this barn somewhere, gentlemen," she blurted without looking at her brother who stood with his mouth open and moving like a fish out of water.

"A young girl," Nancy added, "went missing after a school picnic at Lake Hamilton in 1947, and we have reason to believe that girl's body has been concealed in or near this barn all these years."

"And just who might you young ladies be?" the oldest of the men, a farmer in bib overalls and a plaid cotton shirt asked with a deep furrow in his tanned brow.

"That's my partner in the business and sister, Amelia," Nathan said with irritation in his voice.

"And I'm Nancy Adams with the Briarton Daily News." She extended her hand. "I'm doing a story for the paper on these two and their business. I'm also updating the original story written seventy years ago after Margaret Adkins' disappearance, and this barn seems the likely spot her remains could have been concealed."

The old man scratched his head of thinning gray hair. "I was at that picnic, you know. It was a really good day, as I recall. We were all ready for the school year to be over and just wanted to have some fun."

Nancy stepped forward with her notebook and pen in her hands. "Do you remember seeing Margaret that day, Mr. Mathers?"

"We all called her Peggy," he said with a smile on his florid face. "Leggy Peggy because she had a set of gams that wouldn't quit." He raised a brow. "I was hopin' to get a look at her in a swimsuit that day, but she showed up in a skirt and sweater like most of the other girls and never changed into anything else."

"So, you did see her," Nancy said as she scribbled in her notebook.

"Dad," a younger man said as he took the older man by the arm, "maybe you shouldn't speak to the press if this is some sort of murder investigation on our property."

The old man scowled at his son. "Do you see any police out here, nitwit? If it was an official murder investigation, the damned cops would be swarmin' all over this place and they're not."

"At this point," Nancy said in an authoritative voice, "the paper is just speculating, but we have every belief Margaret Adkins' body is somewhere in that barn and feel bulldozing it at this point would destroy any chance of finding her remains and evidence of her killer or killers."

The old man snorted. "Everyone knows who that would be."

"Who?" Nancy and Amelia said at the same time with their eyes wide.

"A bunch of us saw Peggy go off into the woods with that polished turd Dave Sizemore after they took the group photo for the yearbook," the old man said, "and a few minutes later his drunken lap dog, Keith Hodges, followed after them like he always did."

"And you didn't tell that to the police during their investigation of Margaret's disappearance back in '47?" Amelia asked in an irritated tone.

"Young lady," the elder Mathers said, "you obviously aren't aware of how things worked in Briarton back then. Sizemores and Hodges were untouchable, and you certainly didn't inform on them to the police if you wanted your family to continue doing business here." The old man shrugged. "Anyhow, David told everyone Peggy was a loose-lipped slut who screwed anyone who asked and ran off that day with some guy they'd watched her screw who was passing through town on his way to Chicago." He shrugged. "Who was I to say different?"

Amelia glanced at the barn and her cheeks flamed with rage. "Had you screwed her, Mr. Mathers? It sounds like you wanted to." The old man shook his head in a negative response. "Then maybe you should have cut Peggy some slack and not paid any attention to the guy you called a polished turd."

"There's a very good chance that poor girl's remains are still somewhere in that barn—maybe buried in the dirt floor," Nancy said. "We only need a few more days to conduct the search, sir."

"This is ridiculous," the younger Mathers huffed. "Nobody cares about the seventy-year-old disappearance of a missing small-town slut. This barn is coming down today and that's all there is to it."

The old man's eyes narrowed, and he glared at his son. "I care, Bernard." He whirled his finger in the air. "Load the dozer back up, Herb, and take it home," he yelled to the man by the big yellow machine. "These folks have until next Thursday to finish up here." The old man smiled at Nancy. "If Peggy is here, you have until then to find her. That's the best I can do. That dozer will be back here first thing next Friday morning to knock down what's left of this old heap."

Amelia, Nancy, and Nathan watched the dozer go back on the trailer and the Mathers men follow it away from the old barn in their pickup.

"I don't know what you two were going on about,"

Nathan said, "but I'm sure as hell glad you bought us a few more days. I really wanted these big oak eight by eights to cut down and lathe for furniture. I can't afford to buy new stuff like that."

Amelia grinned. "I could use a new dining room table."

"And I've always wanted a four-poster bed," Nancy added, elbowing Amelia with a broad smile on her face.

Nathan furrowed his brow. "I'll see what I can come up with." He stared back at the remains of the big barn. "Just where do you two think this body is, anyhow?"

"We see Peggy in that little room on the far end," Nancy told him. "You should begin there.

Nathan's mouth fell open and he stared at his sister. "She sees them too?"

"Apparently so," Amelia said with a grin tugging at the corners of her mouth.

She heard her cell phone rang and jogged back to the car where she had it plugged in to charge.

"Hello?"

"Miss Ryan?" a female voice asked.

"Yes, this is Amelia." She didn't intend to go into explaining her name change here on the phone.

"This is Amanda Potter at your grandmother's care facility, Rolling Acres."

Amelia sensed bad news coming and her heart began to pound in her chest. "Yes?"

"I'm afraid I have bad news. We found your grandmother Jennifer O'Connor deceased in her bed this morning."

Amelia's breath caught in her throat. "I was just there yesterday, and she was fine."

"Unfortunately, it happens like that sometimes with the elderly," Mrs. Potter said. "I contacted your mother and she told me to call you as you'd be responsible for making your grandmother's final arrangements. Which funeral home would you like us to contact for you to collect her body?"

It didn't surprise Amelia that her mother wanted to have nothing to do with her mother's final arrangements. "Tully and Gould buried my grandfather and they have all the information. She has a prearranged plan with them, but won't she be going to the coroner's office first to determine what killed her?"

"With people your grandmother's age, Ms. Ryan, the coroner seldom conducts autopsies. She died peacefully in her sleep. Can you not simply leave it at that?"

"I want a goddamned autopsy to tell me how she died," Amelia screamed into the phone. "And I'll be there within the hour to clean her things out of her room."

"That would be much appreciated, Ms. Ryan. We have a long waiting list here at Rolling Acres and could have a new resident in the room tomorrow if you collected Jennifer's things today."

Amelia bet they would too. Tears streamed from her eyes. After hearing her scream, Nathan and Nancy rushed to the Subaru. Amelia got out and stood shaking beside the car.

"What is it, sis?" Nathan asked with concern when he saw her tears.

"Grandma Jen is dead, Bubba," she said with a sob and fell into her big brother's arms.

"What happened? Weren't you just there yesterday?" Nathan asked as he held his sobbing sister.

"Mrs. Potter said she died in her sleep last night."

"A stroke or something?" he asked.

"They didn't know, but I told them to call the damned coroner to find out. She was perfectly healthy when I saw her yesterday and in good spirits."

"Did you call Mom?"

"Our dear mother told Mrs. Potter to call me because I'd be the one making Grandma's final arrangements not her."

"Are you shitting me?" Nathan gasped.

"Nope," Amelia said, wiping her eyes. "I'm on my way over to clean out Grandma's room now. Mrs. Potter said they have a waiting list and want to move someone new in the room tomorrow."

"Fucking vultures," Nathan spat as he wiped his own tears away. "Do you want me to come with you, sis?"

Amelia shook her head as she backed out of Nathan's arms. "I should do this alone, Bubba. Grandma would want it that way."

Nathan nodded in understanding. "You want to talk to her about what happened."

"There might be something she wants to tell us," Amelia muttered, her voice choked with emotion.

Nancy put a hand on Amelia's shoulder. "Go deal with your grandma, Amelia. I'll hitch a ride back into town with Nathan or one of his guys."

"Thanks, Nancy. I'll call you later." Amelia got into the car and started the engine.

Thoughts of her beloved grandmother filled Amelia's head as she drove back into Briarton, and tears slid down her cheeks as she remembered Jenny's request to visit Prairie Road the day before and her inability to grant it. Amelia's anger at her mother neared an explosive point by the time she parked at the home and walked inside Rolling Acres.

She went to the nurses' station. "I'm Amelia O'-Connor and I'm here to clean out my grandmother, Jenny O'Connor's room."

She didn't wait for the slack-faced woman with her nose in a paperback novel to reply and stormed off down the hall to her grandmother's room. Amelia stepped inside the room to find a young man in the blue scrubs of an orderly going through her grand-mother's closet. Drawers from her bedside table had been dumped on the bed and the contents pilfered through.

"Hi, sweetheart," Jenny O'Connor said with a broad smile on her face as she sat on the edge of the bed. Her weightless body made no dent on the mat-tress. "This little piss ant thinks I might have hidden treasure here somewhere," she said with a giggle only Amelia could hear.

"Is there something specific you're looking for?" Amelia asked in a loud, clear voice.

"Huh, what?" the young man gasped as he turned to see Amelia. "I'm supposed to clean out this room for the next resident."

"And that includes pilfering through the former resident's things?" Amelia snapped.

The young man grinned and shrugged. "The crazy old bird is dead," he said, "what does she care?"

Crazy huh? "Get the fuck out of my grandmother's room before I call the police, and have you arrested for burglary," Amelia hissed.

"But Mrs. Potter told me to—"

"Then I'll call the police on Mrs. fucking Potter too. This room has been paid for until the end of the goddamned month and neither you nor anyone else, but her family has any business going through her things."

The young man shut the closet door and scrambled out of the room with the Life Shadow of Jenny O'Connor laughing hysterically on the bed. "I think he pissed his damned pants, Amelia."

Amelia closed the door and sat on the bed beside her grandmother's shadowy form. "What happened, Grandma? You were just fine yesterday."

"Oh," Jenny said with a long sigh, "I thought I could play Jessica Fletcher and draw Sizemore into a damned murder confession. She always made it look so easy."

"Jessica Fletcher?" Amelia didn't recognize the name.

"You know," Jenny said, "Murder, She Wrote. It was our favorite show on Sunday nights when I first got back from Lockwood."

Amelia thought for a minute and then recalled the murder mystery program with Angela Lansbury she and her grandmother watched together on Sunday evenings before Elizabeth had put her in this place.

"You approached Sizemore about killing Margaret Adkins? I asked you not to do that, Grandma."

Jenny grinned. "And he was none too forthcoming about it until he found his way into my room later."

Amelia's mouth fell open. "What happened, Grandma?"

"I'm dead, aren't I?"

"Oh, my lord," Amelia gasped as her head began to spin and her stomach threatened to expel her morning coffee and bagel. "He killed you?"

Jenny's hand brushed Amelia's cheek and sent a

shot of electricity through her body. "if that fool coroner says I died of natural causes, and you don't get justice for me, I'll be spending eternity in this damned room." She smiled sadly at her granddaughter. "Wouldn't that make your damned mother happy?" She brushed a hand over Amelia's tearstained cheek. "Please don't let that happen, Amelia."

"I'll do my best, Grandma." Amelia said as she went to the closet and grinned back at her grandmother. "Now where exactly do you have those treasures hidden?"

Jenny smiled. "You'll find some notebooks in a box with everything I know about Life Shadows, Amelia. Read them and share them with your friend. If she has the gift, she'll need to know things as well."

Amelia bent to look for the notebooks. "And, sweetheart?"

"Yes, Grandma?" she said, turning her head back to the bed.

"Go to Prairie Road and tell your grandfather I'm on my way to find him."

Tears leaked down Amelia's face as she saw the longing in her grandmother's eyes. "I will, Grandma. I know he'll be happy to hear it."

Jenny snorted. "The old coot's gonna say I waited long enough."

Amelia wondered if she should tell her grandmother she'd gone to Prairie Road the day before but couldn't find her grandfather. She decided she wouldn't and continued to pull things from the closet and sort them. Some she would take with her, some she would leave for other residents who could use them, and others would go into the trash.

7

AMELIA LEFT ROLLING ACRES WITH ALL HER grandmother's belongings stuffed into three large gift bags she'd found neatly folded in the closet. She could remember the things she'd brought the old woman in each one for birthdays and Christmases and it broke her heart to realize a human being's life could be carried away with ease in three brightly colored paper bags.

From the home, Amelia drove directly to the coroner's office. It took her nearly an hour to gain entrance into the medical unit to see her grandmother's pale body, lying on a steel table draped with a thin blue paper sheet.

Amelia stepped close with tears in her eyes, bent, and kissed her grandmother's cold forehead. She knew her grandmother's essence remained at Rolling Acres, but her physical body was here. She could kiss her one last time and inhale the scent of her perfume.

"I'm going to say this was a simple heart attack," the doctor told Amelia. "There's no need to defile her body with a messy post-mortem."

Amelia studied her grandmother's serene face and

then noticed something. "How do you explain this bruising on her neck, Doctor Murphy?"

The retired family practitioner who'd given Amelia her pre-school shots walked over to stare at the purple bruising on Jenny's throat. "It's probably explained by her thrashing while in the throes of the heart attack, Amelia, nothing more."

Nothing more, indeed. Amelia gently lifted the lids of her grandmother's eyes. "And what about these red spots in her eyes, doctor? How do you explain that? The crime shows generally say that's a sign of suffocation or strangulation, don't they?"

Doctor Murphy smiled. "I think you're looking for any excuse other than the obvious for your poor grandmother's death, Amelia."

"What are you talking about? She has huge bruises on her throat and hemorrhaging in her eyes. I don't think this was a simple heart attack, Doctor."

"I'm the one who spent years in medical school and decades in practice," Murphy sneered. "Just because you've watched a few episodes of CSI, don't think you're some forensics expert, Amelia and can go over my head with this." He pulled the sheet over Jenny's face. "Your grandmother died of a heart attack in her sleep and that is that. I'll be sending her body over to Gould's for cremation in the morning."

"Cremation?" Amelia gasped. "She's supposed to be buried next to my grandfather at Forest Haven."

"You can plant her ashes there, but Gould only does cremations now. The funeral business has gotten too expensive for coffin burials, Amelia. If she had one of those pre-arranged things, it's for cremation now unless you have several thousand more to toss around just to bury her." Murphy stripped off his rubber gloves and marched out of the examination room.

Amelia needed to speak to her grandmother again. Had she been aware of all this? She called Gould's and spoke with the owner. His family had handled the O'-Connor and Ryan family's final arrangements for decades.

"I'm so sorry to hear about your loss, Miss Ryan," Albert Gould said in a cool voice. "What seem to be your concerns?"

"I'm at the coroner's office and there are some things about my grandmother's body that concern me deeply and Dr. Murphy doesn't want to address them at all."

"Murphy's an old quack with a title behind his name that gives him a little power," Gould sneered. "I'll have a look at her when she gets here tomorrow."

After an hour of conversation, Amelia had promises from the mortuary director to autopsy, photograph, and take samples from the bruising around Jenny's neck and beneath her fingernails for DNA testing. He also assured Amelia that Jenny was fully aware of the cremation and had agreed to it. There would be a small memorial service at the funeral home with an obituary placed in The Daily. She could take the ashes home with her or he would arrange to bury them in Forest Haven with her grandfather if that was what she wanted.

A visit with Sheriff Roy Tate wasn't much more successful than her visit with the coroner. Tate shuffled her off to a deputy who took her statement and then promised to send an investigator to Rolling Acres. She left, feeling depressed, and certain the sheriff's department wouldn't be any more helpful than the coroner.

Amelia drove to Gould's Funeral Home on North Main Street to have a look at her grandmother's contract. Satisfied the man hadn't lied to her, Amelia stepped out into the cloudy afternoon and decided to take a walk, to work off some of the day's frustration. She wasn't ready to return to her empty apartment yet and deal with her overwhelming grief.

She couldn't help but blame herself for Jenny's death at the hands of David Sizemore. Had Amelia not gone to Jenny with questions about Margaret Adkins and David Sizemore, her grandmother would still be alive. Tears ran down Amelia's face as she walked over the cracked, uneven sidewalks in an older section of north Briarton. The houses here were mainly bungalows built before the Depression and most hadn't been updated since the seventies with peeling aluminum lap siding, unkept yards, and older model sedans parked in the drives.

The sound of an old Elvis Presley tune wafted from one particular dark home along with the childish laughter of little girls. Amelia thought it strange and walked up the crumbling concrete steps onto the porch. She saw a sign on the screen door and moved closer to read it. The sign warned of danger. The house had been condemned by the city, and the owner was looking for someone to tear it down. She used the camera feature on her phone to click a picture of the sign to text to Nathan later.

The music and laughter drew Amelia closer and she knocked. When nobody answered, she tried the knob and the door opened. The house smelled musty and stale with lingering aromas of rancid bacon grease and cigarettes. It was empty of furniture and no curtains hung at the smudged windows. Nobody was living in the house, but she followed the sound of the music and laughter through the vacant house to a rear bedroom where she saw two little girls around the ages of seven or eight dancing to Elvis's Jailhouse Rock with wild abandon and laughter that made Amelia smile for the first time that day. They wore their dark hair in pigtails, had on matching sweaters, poodle-skirts, bobby socks, and saddle shoes. They weren't twins, but close in age.

"Hi," Amelia said in a soft voice.

Both little girls stopped dancing, they began to fade, and the music went quiet. "Don't go," Amelia pled, and the shapes of the children began to flicker like the images of an old movie as the hairs on her arms stood up with the same electrical charge she'd experienced at the barn with Peggy. "Who are you girls and what are you doing here all alone?"

The older of the two girls solidified somewhat and took a step toward Amelia. "We're waiting for our Mommy to get here," she said with a nervous glance at her sister. Amelia could see the family resemblances between the two girls upon looking closer.

"Where is your Mommy?"

The younger of the girls shrugged her tiny shoulders. "Daddy left us here and told us to wait," she said in a meek voice. "He was really mad and told us he'd be back with Mommy to join us soon."

Amelia furrowed her brow in confusion. "To join you where?" she asked.

The younger girl pointed at the hardwood floor. "Here," she said. "Daddy said he'd be back with Mommy, but he never brought her, and we've been waiting for a long, long time for them to come back." The little girl began to cry, and her sister took her into her arms.

Blueberry Hill began to play on an invisible record player. "Penny gets really sad," the older girl said as she hugged her weeping sister. "Can you help us find our Mommy?"

Amelia smiled as Fats Domino wailed. "I'll see what I can do, sweetheart," she said, then turned and left the Life Shadows of the girls.

The music changed to a lively Chuck Berry tune and the laughter resumed. Amelia took out her phone and texted Nathan with the information about the house and the address. Would these two little Life Shadows be happier without her interference? Something had obviously happened to their parents, but Amelia had no way of knowing what.

After receiving Nathan's thanks for the lead, Amelia called Nancy. "I've got something for you to investigate, Nancy Drew."

"Another haunted barn?"

"An old house at 1214 Burns Street here in Briarton," she said, "and yes, it's haunted."

Nancy whistled. "Life around you will either make or break my career, Amelia, that's for certain."

Amelia smiled. "The Daily is going to need an obituary for my grandmother," she said with a long sigh. "I'd love for you to write it."

Amelia heard Nancy take a breath. "I'd be honored, Amelia."

"Come over tonight and we'll talk about it over a bottle of wine and dinner. The Grand Opening for the store is this weekend and I have a few finishing touches I need to do."

Nancy giggled. "In other words, you need someone to judge whether or not you have your pictures hung straight."

"I still have so much work to do, and now I have grandma's funeral to deal with on top of all that."

"I'll be over at six, Amelia."

Amelia made a lasagna and salad. The aroma of the lasagna baking attracted Nathan into the shop, and he showed up in the kitchen at the same time as Nancy.

"Sure smells good, sis. You make enough for three?"

"You eat as much as three on your own, Bub," she said with a wink at Nancy, "but yah, I have plenty."

Nathan dropped into one of the chairs. "Good, because I'm starving, and Mom never cooks anymore."

Amelia raised a brow and turned to stare at her brother. "Why? Did that avocado-green monstrosity finally bite the dust?"

Nathan shook his head. "Mom's just not the same since you left."

Amelia snorted as she took the lasagna from the oven to the table. "No one for the drama queen to lord over anymore."

"That looks great, sis," Nathan said and reached for the sizzling cheesy dish with a fork. "Got any parmesan to go on this?"

Amelia smacked his hand. "Of course, I do," she scolded, "but you need to wash up first and wait for me to get everything on the table."

Nathan returned the fork to his plate and got up from the chair with a pout on his handsome face. "Yes, Mom." He marched off to the bathroom with the two women giggling behind him.

"Are all men such babies?" Nancy asked as she opened the bottle of wine.

"When their brains split and fall into their ball sacks at puberty, they stop all mature growth," Amelia said with a sigh as she rolled hot breadsticks off a cookie sheet onto a plate.

"Is that medical fact or just from observations?" Nancy asked with a grin.

"I've been researching it for years and think I'll write a paper on it."

Nancy glanced at the bathroom. "Speaking of writing, Kusak's given me the OK to put together a piece on Sizemore and Hodges' involvement in Margaret Adkins's disappearance. He thinks there's enough there for me to run with."

Hearing Sizemore's name gave Amelia chills. "I wish there was some way I could get the sheriff to listen to me about Sizemore and my grandmother," she said, "but that's never going to happen. He says there's no way an old man in a wheelchair could attack my grandmother in her bed and kill her."

"And the coroner's report says it was natural causes." Nancy filled three glasses with sweet red wine.

"I'm hoping Mr. Gould can remedy that." Amelia took a can of Parmesan cheese from the refrigerator and set it on the table along with bottles of salad dressing before she took her seat at the table. "I think that's about everything."

Nathan came in from the bathroom and filled his plate. "This looks really great, sis. I haven't had home-cooked lasagna in a long time."

"I make it with zucchini from my garden rather than pasta sometimes," Nancy said as she filled her salad plate.

Nathan gave her a look of horror. "Zucchini? You're not a damned vegan, are you?"

Nancy grinned. "I use shredded zucchini in place of spaghetti too."

Nathan grabbed a breadstick and stuffed it into his mouth. "Don't tell me you're one of those no-carb freaks."

Nancy forked up a breadstick of her own. "I love my carbs as much as anyone else," she said, "but my dad had to go on a really strict diet a few years ago or he was going to lose his job at the prison." She used the spatula to serve herself a helping of the lasagna. "I had to learn low-carb recipes, so dad didn't have to go without a lot of the things he liked to eat. Thus," she said with a grin, "zucchini lasagna and spaghetti as well as mashed cauliflower in place of mashed potatoes."

"Cauliflower? Yuck!" Nathan gasped in horror. Both women laughed.

"So," Nancy said in a voice meant to change the subject. "Kusak liked the piece I did on you guys so much he wants me to cover your Grand Opening in a big way."

"That's great, Nancy," Nathan said between bites. "What did you have in mind?"

"If it's all right with the two of you, I thought I'd hang out here with you all day like I was part of the enterprise and get lots of pictures while I took in the reaction of the crowd."

"I hope there's a crowd," Amelia said and sipped her wine.

Nancy smiled at her new friend. "There will be if the buzz I hear around town is anything to go by."

"Do we have everything in order, sis?"

"I don't know. Do you have that futon finished so I can put it on display?"

Amelia had been so impressed with the futon Nathan had made her for the apartment, she'd told him she wanted one for the store as well.

Nathan grinned. "That and the bed you wanted made from those old fence pickets you bought at the swap meet."

Amelia rolled her eyes. "Great now I need to add a twin sized mattress and bedding to my shopping list along with everything we'll need for the barbecue out front.

"Make me a list," Nancy offered, and I can help with the shopping. My mom wanted to make a run up to Costco tomorrow anyhow."

"You see," Nathan said with a smile at Nancy, "she's gonna be a big help around here."

"She already has been," Amelia said with a sigh. "She's going to write Gran's obituary for the Daily."

"Do you have a nice picture of her, sis? I don't think Mom has any."

"I have plenty," Amelia said. "There is even her yearbook photo from that yearbook we got from Grace Adkins."

Nancy sat chewing on her fork. "I've been thinking," the reporter said to Amelia. "It might be fun to put together a story about your grandmother—and you."

"And me?"

"About your special abilities—your abilities to see and talk to the dead." Nancy paused. "How it was you who discovered Margaret in that barn and got this whole ball rolling."

Nathan dropped his fork on his empty plate. "I

don't think that's a very good idea. My mom's not going to want that craziness about our family in the newspapers."

Nancy's face fell at his words and her bottom lip began to quiver. "You think people with the ability to see and interact with the dead are crazy? I could see Margaret Adkins, and I certainly interacted with her."

Amelia saw tears welling in the young woman's eyes. "Nathan's saying our mother wouldn't like it, Nancy. She's the one who thinks it's craziness, not Nathan."

Nathan's eyes flashed to his sister with a look of gratitude. "I think a story about Grandma Jen, explaining her abilities would be great, Nancy, but maybe about Grandma Jen only, and after the opening of the store when things have settled down a little."

Amelia smiled at her brother. Nice recovery, Bubba.

8

———

THE DAY OF THE GRAND OPENING WAS RAINY BUT didn't keep the nosey of Briarton away.

Amelia wore a sleeveless embroidered denim dress with her red hair done up in a blue country bandana and white cowboy boots on her feet. She looked every bit the red neck entrepreneur. Nathan with his gas grill set up on the sidewalk out front served free hotdogs. Nancy in jeans and a cowboy hat offered bags of chips, potato salad, and slaw for people to enjoy with cans of iced soda. People sat at tables and benches Nathan had built from the barn wood reclaimed from the Mathers' barn. He'd set them up in front of the store and kept the people outside with their food until they'd finished.

The day started slow, but by noon, the rain had cleared and the crowd, attracted by the free food and a promised break in the boredom of a Briarton Saturday soon filled the freshly decorated little store. Rain splashed the sidewalk a few times during the day, but by the time Nathan shut down his grill, Nancy cleared the tables, and Amelia swept up, Barnwood Builders was a proven success on the Briarton Square.

"Renting you this place was a good idea after all," Brian Smith, her landlord said when he stopped in to visit.

Amelia smiled. "You had reservations?"

"Dan Cramer wanted to put a video game store in here and I almost went with it." He stared around at Nathan's furniture and grinned. "This is a much better fit with the community." He stood. "Take me up and show me what you did with that wreck of an apartment."

At one point, Amelia glanced up to see a man smiling as he read the card she'd attached to the back of one of her wallpaper plaques. Amelia didn't see only the Life Shadows of horrible events in a place. Many times, she caught the snippets of everyday life in the buildings they tore down. In this particular house she'd seen the family at a dinner after the woman had put up the wallpaper. She told her guests the pattern reminded her of apples hanging from a tree in Summer. From his highchair, her young son announced he thought it looked like the turds hanging from his dog Buddy's behind. Amelia had thought it hilarious and sketched the scene for the card she taped to the back. She called them the Life Moments of the buildings and tried to have a card for every piece she and Nathan created. She was having a difficult time with the cards for things built from the Mathers' barn. Perhaps she would just use a sketch of Peg done from her yearbook photo and call it good.

The man turned to Amelia with tears in his eyes. "How could you have known that?" He clutched the plaque to his chest. "How could you have known my Buddy was a wire-haired Terrier? It was so long ago." He purchased every piece Amelia had on the wall made with that wallpaper and card. "Mom's gone, Buddy's gone, and now the house is gone, but with these I can give my kids a little piece of my childhood I thought was gone forever." It had been one of the brightest points of Amelia's day.

As she'd been dressing the bed Nathan had built from the white picket fencing, Amelia had seen a silky gold cocker spaniel running and barking along the fenced yard, and a young woman, calling him Oliver. She'd sketched up a card and called the piece Oli's bed. A couple had purchased it for their daughter's room, promising the little girl they would do their best to find her a dog that looked like the one on the card. Amelia was glad she could pass along Life Moments like those to the people who purchased their creations.

The only damper on the day had been the visit from Elizabeth and Matthew Ryan.

"What the hell is that?" Elizabeth had screeched, pointing at the stenciled barn wood sign above the door. She pushed her way inside, demanding to see this Amelia O'Connor, proprietress of the store.

Amelia stood at the register with customers. "Good afternoon, Mother," she said and then thanked the customers for their large purchase.

"I can't be your damned mother," Elizabeth hissed at Amelia, "because my name is Ryan and not O'Connor."

Amelia shrugged. "That's your choice, I suppose, but I'm not ashamed of the O'Connor name or the gifts that come along with it."

"Gifts, my ass," Elizabeth spat. "Crazy is not a gift. It's a goddamned curse, and if that's what you want for your life then that's fine with me, Amelia, but don't think you can come running back home when it rears up to bite you in the ass and this little junk store of yours falls down around your ears along with your poor brother's." She turned and stormed back out the door.

"Your mother?" Nancy asked, poking her head in after Elizabeth and Matthew had driven away.

"Sorta remind you of the Tasmanian Devil from the cartoons whirling in on a tornado, grumbling and snarling?" Amelia asked as she righted a display her mother had knocked over.

Nancy grinned and winked. "Yah, sorta."

"You all right, sis?" Nathan asked when he brought her a hotdog and a can of cold root beer. "Dad said the place looked really great, and he was impressed with the crowd of people here."

Amelia snorted. "And Mom called me a crazy O'-Connor bitch who was gonna come running back home with her tail between her legs."

Nathan grinned and patted his sister's head. "You should have been expecting that, sis."

She smiled at her brother and bit into the hotdog he'd dressed with relish, onions, and mustard the way she liked. Nancy took lots of pictures of the busy store and the smiling people leaving with bags filled with merchandise. Her article and the glossy color photos filled the Briarton Daily News Sunday Supplement, and Nathan bought several copies and cut out the ones featuring his smiling face. He and Nancy were officially dating now, and Amelia couldn't have been happier for the two of them.

Although there were no hotdogs the following day, business at Barnwood Builders was brisk with plenty of out-of-town traffic. Nancy's supplement had been picked up by some affiliate papers in their part of the state, and customers had driven in to visit the new store.

Her cellphone rang just before five. She saw Nathan's number and smiled. "Calling to check on business, Bub?" she asked cheerfully. "Well, it's great and I took another order for a table and benches and," she added, "the futon sold too, so I'm gonna need another."

"You and Nancy need to get out here to the barn right away, sis," Nathan said and disconnected without commenting on her news.

Her brother's tone frightened Amelia. The last customers were exiting, and she followed them and locked the door. She turned to Nancy, who'd been helping her all day in Nathan's absence. His crew had wanted to finish the barn and he'd reluctantly agreed because the weather reports were calling for more rain in the days to come. "Nathan says we need to get to the barn."

"What?" Nancy asked with her blue eyes wide. "Why?"

Amelia shrugged as she switched off the lights. "No idea. He just said for the both of us to get there on the double."

"All right," Nancy said as she followed Amelia out the back door and got into the electric-blue Subaru Forester parked in the alley.

They drove without speculating and were surprised to see police vehicles parked around what remained of the old barn. The roof was gone and only a few of the large support beams remained. "Oh, wow," Nancy said under her breath and began digging into her bag for her notebook and pen. She slipped her camera around her neck and they got out of the car.

"This is a crime scene, ladies," a deputy in an ill-fitting brown county uniform said as he stopped them at a band of yellow plastic crime scene tape. "You need to return to your vehicle and exit the scene."

"Let me guess," Amelia said, "they found the long-dead remains of a young woman in that barn."

"Her name is Margaret Adkins and she was murdered in May of 1947," Nancy added.

The deputy's face paled. "How do you know that?"

Amelia grinned at Nancy. "If we told you we'd have to kill you, deputy." Amelia stepped close to the wide-eyed uniformed man.

"May we please go in now?"

The deputy swallowed hard and then began speaking into a mike attached to his collar. "The sheriff says you can go in," he said and stepped aside to give Amelia and Nancy a wide berth as they passed.

"You're an evil bitch," Nancy said with a giggle.

"So, my mother keeps telling me," Amelia said with a grin as they stepped into the small space crowded with people. The sidewalls were gone as well as the rotted floor of the loft overhead and the rafters where the swallows had nested. Amelia wondered where the birds would go and if they'd had young in those mud nests.

Nathan rushed to their side. "We were prying up the last of that floor," he said, nodding to the raised platform, "and that's where we found her."

They heard the wailing of a siren and soon an ambulance marked with Coroner on the side parked near the barn and Doctor Murphy got out. He saw Amelia and frowned.

She was certain the old doctor wasn't happy because Mr. Gould had contradicted his findings and brought in another examiner to have her grandmother's death ruled a homicide rather than one of natural causes. Murphy like other doctors, suffered from a serious god-complex and didn't like being contradicted.

"What do you have here?" Murphy asked the sheriff when he came in, ignoring Amelia as he plowed by to what remained of the platform.

Amelia and Nancy followed along beside Nathan. Between two joists were heaped dusty bones. Clumps of thick brown hair clung to the skull and Amelia had no doubt they'd found the remains of Margaret Adkins. She was surprised the weeping girl was not present.

Murphy picked up the skull and studied it. "Female Caucasian late teens to early twenties," he said, "dead I'd say for a good fifty years."

"Margaret Adkins," Amelia said in a loud clear voice. "Fifteen years old and dead since May 7of 1947."

Murphy glared at Amelia. "How can you possibly know that, Miss Ryan?"

Nancy stepped forward. "Because I'm with the Briarton Daily News and we've reopened and have been investigating Margaret Adkins' disappearance after a school picnic at Lake Hamilton."

"And would you like to venture a guess as to the cause of death, Miss Ryan?" Potter sneered. "Since you seem to be psychic and know it all."

"Ligature strangulation with a belt," Amelia said with confidence.

The old doctor's mouth fell open. "How could you possibly know that?" he demanded.

Nathan bent and lifted something concealed in the

dusty space with the bones. "A belt like this?" he asked as he held up a moldy two-inch wide strip of leather dangling from a fancy monogramed buckle, the silver tarnished to black with age and exposure to the decaying body of Margaret Adkins.

Nancy snapped photos as Nathan held up the buckle. "What's that buckle say on it?" she asked.

Nathan studied the oval buckle. "It looks like DAS," he said, "in fancy scrollwork." He whistled at its weight as he hefted it. "I'd bet it was damned expensive back then."

"David Allan Sizemore," Amelia said. "The same David Sizemore living at the nursing home where my grandmother was murdered after she asked him what he knew about Margaret's disappearance and murder."

"That's ridiculous and libelous, Miss Ryan. David Sizemore is one of the pillars of this community and you and your grandmother are—"

"Are what?" Nathan, with his muscular six-foot-four-inch frame towering over the chubby doctor demanded.

"It's common knowledge in Briarton, Mr. Ryan, that the O'Connor women have always suffered from delusions and your grandmother in particular spent the majority of her adult life in psychiatric facilities—put there I might add by her own daughter to protect the community from her psychotic ravings." He glanced at Amelia and grinned. "It seems the batshit-crazy hasn't fallen far from the tree, has it Miss Ryan or is it Miss O'Connor now?" He began to chuckle along with the sheriff and the gathered deputies.

Nathan drew back his fist and punched the sneering doctor in the face, sending the old man to sprawl on the dirty floor. "My sister and grandmother are psychic, not psychotic, you arrogant, fucking quack."

Nancy grabbed Amelia's hand as she gave Nathan a smile for his heroism. "I think I love that man," she whispered into Amelia's ear.

"Me too," Amelia said, returning Nancy's smile.

———

TOM HODGES WAS EATING his Sunday supper when his cell phone chimed with a call.

"I hope you're not going to answer that during supper, Tom," his wife said with her lip curled in a disapproving snarl.

Tom took the phone from his pocket. "It might be important," he said and swiped the screen to answer. "This is Tom."

"And this is Bob Kusak," the voice on the other end of the phone said. "My reporter just called from that barn out by old Lake Hamilton," he said. "They just found the body of that girl or what's left of her body after seventy years."

"Oh, lord," Tom gasped, almost dropping the phone into his half-eaten plate of food. "What's going to happen now?"

"She's got a damned story now, Tom," Kusak spat, "and she's going to write it for all it's worth."

Tom made a soft chuckle into the phone. "Just because the little bitch writes it," he sneered, "it doesn't mean you have to print it, Bob."

"The Daily is part of a multi-paper consortium now, Tom. If I don't print it, one if not all the others will. This is a big story in a small town, Tom. There's no way I can keep wraps on it now. There's a damned body for Christ's sake."

"Just do what you can," Tom said and disconnected.

"What's going on, Thomas?" his wife asked when she saw the look of concern on her husband's face.

Tom Hodges ran his hand through his thinning hair. "How do you feel about selling out here in Briarton and moving down to Lake of the Ozarks?"

9

———————

JENNIFER O'CONNOR'S FUNERAL WAS AN INTIMATE affair at Tully and Gould's Funeral Home with Amelia and Nathan the only ones representing the family and a few acquaintances attracted by Nancy's well-written obituary in the Daily.

Amelia kept hoping her mother and father would come through the door, but they never did, and by the end of the short service, she seethed with rage.

Nathan, wearing a black western-cut jacket, jeans, and cowboy boots held her hand as they stood in the receiving line before a table set with their grandmother's ashes, photographs of Jenny, her late husband Ned, and her grandchildren. Nancy in a classic black shift stood on the other side of Amelia, who also wore a black, comfortable skirt and sweater she'd owned for years and reserved for funerals.

"Mom's stubborn, Amelia," Nathan whispered into her ear, "but I'm sure she's grieving in her own way."

"Yah," Amelia hissed, "probably with a celebratory barbecue in the back yard."

"Speaking of celebrating," he said, "I'm taking Nancy out to dinner to celebrate her article in The

Daily about Margaret Adkins, her disappearance, and the recovery of her remains." He squeezed his sister's hand. "You should come. Steaks at Applebee's on me."

"Please join us, Amelia," Nancy begged. "You deserve a break after today.

The Saturday evening crowd at Applebee's was loud and Amelia's head ached from crying. She would really rather have gone home, changed into a cotton gown, crawled into her comfortable bed, and read a book, but Nancy deserved her spot in the limelight. Not only had her story appeared in The Briarton Daily, but in seven other papers owned by the news company.

Kusak had balked at printing the story, accusing David Sizemore and Keith Hodges of murdering the girl, but he couldn't deny Nancy's first-hand eyewitness reports of people having seen Sizemore and Hodges leave with the girl at the picnic and return without her.

Sizemore, when Nancy interviewed him at Rolling Acres, repeated his 1947 story that Margaret Adkins was a Rosie Roundheels who would lie down and spread her legs for any boy or man who asked, and after having sex with a strange man in front of him and Keith Hodges, had gone off with him to escape her abusive father. Sizemore denied any knowledge of how Margaret's body or his belt ended up in the barn and refused to answer any more questions after the first few Nancy had asked. He'd feigned heart pains in a ridiculous parody of Red Fox and his nursing assistant had ordered her out.

Amelia, Nancy, and Nathan had attended Margaret's funeral with Grace and Thomas Adkins the day before Jennifer's at the same mortuary.

"My mom says we should write a book about this," Nancy said as they sipped Buds and waited for their steaks.

"At least your mom is supportive," Amelia said.

Nancy smiled. "She's doing an Ancestry search to see if we might be related to the O'Connor family somehow since I seem to have the same abilities as you and your grandmother."

Nathan slammed his bottle on the table. "Please tell her to stop, babe. I don't want to find out I've been sleeping with my damned cousin."

Nancy and Amelia began to laugh.

"I suppose you all find this situation amusing," a man in his fifties dressed in a suit and tie said as he stalked up to their table.

"Excuse me?" Amelia said. "This is a private dinner."

He pointed at Nancy. "And this bitch has violated my family's privacy with her unfounded accusations about my father, his friend, and that dead slut they found out by the lake."

"This is Tom Hodges," Amelia said, "Keith Hodges' son."

"My dad just died, and I don't appreciate you slandering his good name with your damned lies."

"Not one word I wrote was a lie, Mr. Hodges," Nancy said coolly. "Mr. Kusak checked and rechecked every person I interviewed for verification and found every word I wrote substantiated by those witnesses. Your father was one of the last people seen with Margaret Adkins on the day she disappeared and was actually murdered."

"Just because he screwed some dirty little slut in a

barn when he was a kid doesn't mean he had anything to do with killing the little bitch."

"It may be circumstantial," Nancy said with a raised brow, "but lots of murder cases are made on less circumstantial evidence than we have on your father and Sizemore and I think this one will be too at least in the court of public opinion."

They all looked around the quieted room to see people staring at their table. "If I see or hear my father's name brought up in association with this bull-shit case again," Hodges hissed, pointing at the three at the table, "I'll sue all of you, Robert Kusak, and the damned newspapers for libel and defamation of character."

Amelia's phone rang. She answered without looking at the caller ID. "Hello, this is Amelia. How may I help you?"

"You can help me," Elizabeth Ryan's shrewish voice screamed in her ear, "by putting an end to this ridiculous O'Connor craziness and apologizing to that poor man for dragging his poor dead father's name through the mud."

Amelia's eyes darted around the crowded restaurant to see if her mother was there. When she didn't see Elizabeth, she looked for any of her friends who might have called to report Tom Hodges' rant at their table. She grinned when she saw one of her mother's book club friends sitting nearby with her phone in her hand.

"I have no idea what the fuck you're talking about, lady," Amelia snapped with bottled rage as she discon-nected and turned off her phone.

"Who was that?" Nathan asked.

"Nobody of any significance at all," Amelia said and dropped the phone into her pocket.

"Can you believe the gall of that man?" Nancy said as they watched Tom Hodges stalk away, grab his wife by the arm, and drag her out of Applebee's.

"He's a real sweetheart," Nathan said. "But do you think he can cause you any real trouble with that talk about lawsuits?"

"The papers have attorneys for that," Nancy said, "and like I told the bastard, Kusak wouldn't have printed anything about the two guys with their names without verifying my sources first." She squeezed Nathan's hand as she smiled at Amelia. "You two probably shouldn't make any public statements, though. Just to be on the safe side."

Nathan made the pretense of zipping his lips. "Don't worry about me, sweetheart. My lips are sealed. How about you, Amelia?"

Amelia grinned at her brother's use of the endearing term for Nancy and the fact he'd admitted their sexual involvement. "I'm only talking to one reporter and she's sitting right here."

Nancy smiled. "I'm glad to hear you're my exclusive source. I checked into that house on Burns and there might be something there."

"Oh, lord," Nathan groaned. "I just signed the contract to take it down. Please don't tell me there are Life Shadows there too."

"What did you find?" Amelia asked, ignoring her groaning brother, and emptied her beer.

Nancy took her notebook from her bag and flipped through the pages. "In 1958 a woman and her two little girls went missing from that address."

"That would fit with the time period I witnessed,"

Amelia said with a glance across the table at Nathan. "They were dressed in poodle skirts and dancing to Elvis." She grinned at her brother's scowling face and added, "Presley not Costello."

———

TOMMY HODGES SAT in the Briarton Diner, the last eating establishment left on the downtown Square, waiting for Sheriff Tate to arrive for their lunch appointment. The waitress filled his cup with coffee.

"You waiting for someone else, Tommy?" she asked with a coy smile.

Tom appreciated the girl's perky tits in her tight sweater and had even enjoyed a roll in the sack with her once or twice, but he didn't need some two-bit diner slut knowing his business. That bitch from the newspaper was already causing him enough trouble with her lies about his dad and old man Sizemore.

"I'm waiting for Sheriff Tate, Cindy," he snapped. "Now run along and bring him coffee when he gets here."

Cindy walked away as Roy Tate came striding into the diner. He took off his hat and joined Tom with a smile on his face that reminded him of a bullfrog. "What's this all about, Tom?" the sheriff asked. "Lunch is nice, but I've got work to do too." He turned to the counter and called, "Bring me some coffee, sweet cheeks."

"I want to know what you intend to do about this so-called reporter at the Daily who's spreading lies around town about my dad and Dave Sizemore."

The sheriff raised a bushy brow. "You so sure they are lies, Tommy? I recall having your old man in the drunk tank one night and he kept sayin' something over and over about him and Sizemore and a girl in a barn. That wouldn't happen to be the girl would it?"

"My dad had a sickness; Roy and he couldn't shake it." Tom swallowed some coffee. "But he's dead now and I don't think it's right that some little bitch who isn't even from Briarton can go writing lies about him in the Daily."

The sheriff shrugged his broad shoulders. "It's a free fucking country with a free fucking press, Tommy. If you want Kusak to put a muzzle on his bitch, take it up with him and not me." The sheriff's eyes settled on the pretty waitress. "I'd sure like to tap that." He turned back to the frowning businessman. "If you want to make Kusak crawl, file a damned lawsuit, Tommy. He's scared shitless of those damned lawyers and would do anything not to see the inside of a courtroom."

Tom Hodges stood and tossed a twenty on the table. "So, all that cash I dumped into your campaign fund was just wasted?" He walked away with a scowl on his face.

The sheriff snatched up the twenty and stuffed it into his shirt pocket with a grin. "Bring me a double cheeseburger and fries, sweet cheeks, with one of your big chocolate malts to go with it."

10

Nathan and Amelia were served with papers at the store a week after the incident in Applebee's with Hodges.

They were being sued for slander and defamation of character by the Hodges as well as the Sizemore families. Nancy called later to say she and the paper had been served as well. Kusak had told her to server her ties with the Ryans until the suits had been settled, but Nancy had told him to forget about it. She refused to end her relationship with Nathan and saw way too many good stories in her future to do something stupid like walking away from a stupendous, if unusual, source.

"Goddamnit, Amelia," Nathan yelled as he stormed around the store with the papers clutched tight in his fist. "This is all your damned fault."

"My fault?" Amelia yelled back. "I didn't kill anybody."

"Mom's right," he hissed, "this is all just craziness and now you've dragged Nancy into it, and she could lose the job she's fought so hard for because of it."

"That's not fair, Bubba," Amelia said in her own

defense. "I didn't force Nancy to write anything, and it's not my fault she's gifted like I am."

Nathan dropped into a chair and ran a hand through his thick hair. "I'm beginning to agree with Mom on this, sis. It's more of a damned curse than a gift." He pounded his fist on the wooden arm of the chair. "If you hadn't provoked Hodges' son in that restaurant we wouldn't be in this shit with lawsuits. He wants to take the damned business, Amelia. Mom is right about this. It's all craziness and we're going to lose everything we've worked for because of it."

"Grandma says mom—"

"Grandma's dead, Amelia," Nathan bellowed. "She doesn't say anything anymore."

Nathan would know their grandmother had plenty to say if he had the gift, but he didn't. He couldn't see or hear the dead.

Tears of frustration filled Amelia's eyes. She'd always expected to fight with her mother about this, but Nathan had always been on her side. How could he turn on her now?

She went to the door, flipped the deadbolt, and turned over the sign to read Closed. "You're right, Bubba," Amelia said with a deep sigh, "I'm just another crazy O'Connor bitch." She threw up her arms in defeat. "And I'm done. I'll find another apartment and you can run this business any way you see fit. I'm more of a hinderance than a help." Amelia straightened a frame on the wall. "Turn off the lights before you split and lock the back door. I'll start looking for a new place tomorrow."

"What?" she heard Nathan gulp as she stomped up the stairs and slammed the door to her apartment.

Amelia went to her stainless steel side-by-side refrigerator and took out a bottle of sweet, red wine. She filled a glass and dropped onto her bed.

"That bad, huh?" Jenny O'Connor said as her Life Shadow materialized to settle on the bed beside Amelia. "I wish I could have a snort of that." Jenny had been regular company since Amelia had brought her ashes home from the mortuary and set them along with photos on her dresser.

Amelia offered her grandmother the glass. "Be my guest."

"I'd rather have a shot of Jack Daniels," Ned O'-Connor said as he joined his family.

"How did you get away from Prairie Road, Grandpa?" Amelia gasped at the sight of her grandfather, who now looked two decades younger than his wife.

"I've just been waiting for her, while she took her good sweet time," he said, nodding to Jenny.

"I guess I'm going to need to update those notebooks of yours, Grandma."

The old woman shrugged. "I never said it was an exact science."

"Why the long puss, sweetie?" her grandfather asked.

"The Hodges and Sizemores are suing us for telling lies and Nathan is blaming me."

Ned got to his feet. "Where is that boy? Now that I've found my legs, I think I'm gonna go have words with a few people around here."

Jenny put her arm around her husband. "Let's begin with that hard-headed daughter of yours, Ned."

"Nah," Ned said with a grin and a good-natured wink at Amelia. "I was thinkin' about throwin' a good scare into that bastard Sizemore." He kissed Amelia's cheek. "Then we'll go visit Lizzie and rattle a few chains in her attic."

Amelia smiled at her grandfather. "Mom probably won't even notice, but Sizemore has a bad heart and you'll probably kill him, Grandpa."

"That's all right," Ned said. "That'd just put us on an even playin' field for a change."

Amelia wondered if that were true. Would an O'-Connor and a Sizemore be on an even playing field in death? Was that possible in Briarton? Ned O'Connor rested in the ground beneath a simple granite tombstone while the Sizemores rested in a fancy mausoleum in Forest Haven Cemetery. Was that an even playing field?

"Don't fret over it, Amelia," she heard her grandmother whisper, "Ned is as big a blowhard in death as he was in life, but I love him for it all the same."

"Are you gonna let him haunt Sizemore at Rolling Acres?"

Jenny grinned. "You bet I am and that Potter bitch too."

Amelia smiled. "Good."

"And don't worry about Nathan, sweetheart. Your brother will come around. He has a woman with a good head on her shoulders by his side now. She'll set him right about things or slap the piss out of him."

"She thinks we might be related."

Jenny grinned. "Her father's mother was a Killian a few times removed from our ancestry, but a Killian none the less," she said with a wink. "Killian was my maiden name as well."

Amelia's mouth fell open. "Then the gift didn't come from the O'Connors and Mom got it wrong?"

"O'Connor was my married name, not my birth

name. Women carry the gene for the gift," she said, "and occasionally it can be passed through a male child to his female offspring. The gift isn't strong in Nancy, but it's likely to be tremendous in the child she's carrying with Killian blood on both sides of the gene pool."

"Nancy is—"

Likely to give birth on or around St. Bridget's Day."

"Oh, my lord," Amelia gasped.

"Be a good girl and don't give it away," Jenny said with a giggle before taking Ned by the hand and vanishing.

Amelia's phone rang. She dug it out of her pocket and grinned when she saw Nancy's name on the screen. "Hey, Nancy Drew, what's up?"

"I guess Nathan told you about me and the paper being sued."

"Oh, yah," she said. "They're suing us too. Nate's worried we won't be able to afford the lawyers, and Mom and Dad will get drawn into it because we were living with them when all this started."

"Not to worry," she said. "Kusak is pissed as hell and the consortium is going to pick up all of our legal fees."

"Really?"

"Yep, and your guy at the mortuary sent off your grandmother's DNA samples to a private lab a friend of his owns in Chicago for analysis."

"Where does that leave us with Margaret's murder?"

"I'm working a few angles," Nancy said.

"Angles?"

"Wanna get together for greasy burgers, fries, and a beer?"

"I'm working on a bottle of red as we speak," Amelia said.

"Sounds good," Nancy said. "Red is great paired with beef."

Amelia giggled. "Come on over. I'll call in an order if you can pick it up."

"Will do," she said.

Amelia phoned in an order to Red Robin for two big burgers and their famous fries and campfire sauce for dipping. She knew she wouldn't be stepping on the scale for a few days but didn't care.

Nancy arrived loaded with a sack from Red Robin and her leather satchel stuffed with papers. Over dinner they discussed the latest strategy for bringing down David Sizemore and the late Keith Hodges by association.

"Who'd have thought I'd be putting so much effort into going after a man in his late eighties for a seventy-year-old murder," Nancy said as she sipped her wine.

"He wasn't in his eighties when he murdered Margaret Adkins."

Nancy wiped her mouth and frowned. "I only wish Hodges was still here. I can't help but feel he got away easy."

"I don't know about that," Amelia said with a sigh. "I've been doing some digging too, and that man spent his adult life wallowing in guilt. He drowned himself in alcohol for some reason, and I don't buy what he saw in Korea as that reason."

"I hope you don't want me to go easy on him, Amelia. For all we know, it was Hodges stuffing his penis down Margaret's throat that killed her and not Sizemore's belt."

"We know that, Nancy, but there's no way to prove it now."

"Sizemore might throw his dead buddy under the bus if we press him hard enough."

Amelia furrowed her brow. "That would put the story out there," she said, "but there's no way to prove it now. All the medical examiner had was bones. The hyoid was fractured and that means strangulation, but from an external source like Sizemore's belt not asphyxiation from having a penis stuffed down her throat."

"Kusak's been all over me to nail the bastards in the press," Nancy said with a grin.

"So much for the old buddy network sticking together through thick and thin," Amelia said.

Nancy smiled. "All they had to do was say lawsuit and Kusak was out for bear." Nancy nodded to her stuffed satchel. "He's had me going through all the photos I collected."

"Find anything of merit?"

"Only the smoking belt," Nancy said with an impish grin.

Nancy pulled out a draft copy of the article she'd put together. She told Amelia Kusak planned to run it in Sunday's paper. There were photos from the picnic taken in front of the school bus just after the group arrived at Lake Hamilton.

Amelia studied the photo of laughing and smiling teens. "Everyone looks happy." She pointed to a girl standing alone in the second row. "There's our girl."

"And there are our killers," Nancy said as she pointed, using a fry, to two young men hugging one another. "Notice Sizemore's pants."

"You mean the big, over-the-top silver belt buckle?"

"That's the one." Nancy then flipped through the pasted-up article until she came to another photo. "This one came directly from the yearbook," she said. Below the photo it read: The end of another great year at Briarton High. It was the same group of kids at the end of the picnic. They were sunburned, and some wore their swimming suits.

Amelia studied the photo. "There's no Margaret in this one."

Nancy pointed to Sizemore who stood grinning beside Hodges who wasn't. Keith Hodges looked as though he wanted to cry. "No belt either," Nancy said with a grin. "Margaret and the belt are both missing from this photo, and we now know where they were."

Amelia glanced up to see her grandmother staring down at the photo with a smile on her face. "Jessica Fletcher would be proud," Amelia said with a wink.

"Who?" Nancy said, jerking her head up to stare at Amelia.

"Jessica Fletcher from Murder, She Wrote."

Nancy screwed her face up in confusion. "That old TV show?"

"Grandma and I loved it."

"So did I." Nancy emptied her glass. "We could do that, you know."

"Do what?" Amelia asked. "Write murder mysteries?"

"My mom is right." Nancy filled her glass again. "She says the two of us could have a great thing going here."

"What sorta great thing?" She took the glass from

Nancy. "I don't even think you're supposed to be drinking right now, Nancy Drew."

"What?" Nancy gave her a confused stare. "Mom says the book about this case will sell like hotcakes and when we figure out what happened to those two little girls on Burns that book will sell too."

Amelia furrowed her brow as she began cleaning up their dinner mess. "We're writing books now?"

"Mom says we should."

"What does Nathan say?"

Nancy leaned her head back on the couch cushion with a dreamy look on her face and mumbled, "Nathan says I'm crazy and must have O'Connor blood in my veins somewhere."

"Killian blood," Amelia said as she draped a soft throw over Nancy and lifted her legs up on the futon. "The crazy comes from our Killian blood."

"My grandmother was a Killian," Nancy muttered as she snuggled into the pillow with her eyelids drooping.

"So was mine," Amelia said as she carried empty plates and wine glasses into the kitchen area.

Her phone chimed with a text. It was from Nathan: Looking for Nancy. Have you seen her?

Amelia: She's here. Spending the night. Had dinner and drinks. Maybe too many drinks.

Nathan: Thanks sis. Think she needed a break. Did she seem OK to you?

Amelia: Caught up in her story for Kusak.

Nathan: She's working too hard.

Amelia: It's her calling.

Nathan: Thanks sis. Sorry I was a dick today.

Amelia: Good night, Bubba.

Amelia plugged in her phone and got ready for

bed. She wondered if either Nancy or Nathan had any idea they were going to be parents yet. Elizabeth was going to have a cow over that. A daughter seeing ghosts was one thing, but an illegitimate grandchild was a whole other ball of wax.

Jenny materialized on her bedside as Amelia dozed. "I'm sorry, Grandma," she mumbled and reached for her grandmother's hand.

"What do you have to be sorry for, child?"

"I wanted to get justice for you, but I don't know how." Amelia brushed a tear from her cheek. "You're going to be stuck on this plane if I can't figure out a way to get Sizemore for your murder too." She took a deep breath. "There has to be some evidence in that room somewhere."

"At least you got me out of that damned room your mother stuck me in," Jenny said, "and I'll be forever grateful to you for that. If you hadn't brought me home, I'd never have been reunited with your grand-father and that's all I've ever really wanted."

Amelia thought for a minute. "Can you show me what happened to you the way Margaret showed us what happened to her?"

Jenny furrowed her brow. "I don't know. I've never tried."

"Well, give it a shot," Amelia urged.

After a few minutes, Amelia's head began to spin, and her room transformed from that of her apartment to her grandmother's in Rolling Acres. She no longer lounged in her queen-size bed, but Jenny's narrow hospital bed.

The only light in the room came through the slightly open Venetian blinds on the window—Jenny's window at Rolling Acres and not Amelia's drapery clad windows looking out on the Square.

Jenny/Amelia looked up as the heavy door to the hall opened and a dark figure crept in. Amelia knew who it must be, but Jenny was confused. "Who's there?" Jenny's voice croaked from Amelia's throat.

The figure came closer until the face of David Sizemore leered down from above Jenny. "Did you really think I was going to let you get away with smearing my good name with questions about that little slut, you crazy Irish scum?" David Sizemore, smelling of cigarette smoke, coughed and spat in Jenny's face. He pulled the blanket aside and crawled atop Jenny in the narrow bed. "I should fuck your ass the way I fucked hers," he cackled, "but I fear my old prostrate has failed me and my screwing days are long over."

Amelia could feel the fear and anger building in her grandmother. Jenny wiped at the spittle on her face and flung it with disgust at the wall. "Get the hell off me, Sizemore," Jenny hissed as she tried to push the man off her bed. He held tight to the headboard, however and she couldn't budge him.

"Fucking Irish trash," Sizemore hissed as he put his hands around Jenny's neck and began to squeeze. He began to grind his stiff crotch over her belly and Amelia could see him licking his lips. "Maybe this old dick has one more cum left in it after all." Sizemore rutted atop Jenny's body as he strangled her.

Amelia felt her grandmother's hyoid bone pop with the pressure of Sizemore's grip and her eyesight blur as Jenny O'Connor lost her ability to suck air into her lungs.

"Is that really what you wanted to experience?"

Jenny asked, once again at her granddaughter's side on the queen-size bed in the apartment.

"It's exactly what I wanted to experience," Amelia said with a cough, rubbing at her throat and the vanished fingers of David Sizemore. "I think it's exactly what we needed to get that murdering bastard once and for all."

11

———

Amelia stormed into the sheriff's office the following morning with a blurry-eyed Nancy at her side.

"What are we doing here, Amelia?" Nancy asked.

"Getting some justice for my grandmother."

Sheriff Roy Tate saw them walk in and rolled his puffy eyes. "Haven't you two girls bitten off more than you can chew already with that nonsense out at the old lake?"

"I want to know what you've found in the investigation of my grandmother's murder, sheriff?" Amelia demanded.

"According to our esteemed coroner, Miss Ryan, your grandmother died of natural causes and not murder," he said in a snide tone.

"And you know good and well those findings were overturned by another medical examiner, sheriff. My grandmother was murdered, and I want to know what you're going to do about it."

Tate put his hands on his broad hips, bent, and grinned in Amelia's face. "People can't pick and choose a medical examiner until they get a finding they like, Miss Ryan. Dr. Murphy is the elected Medical Examiner of this county and his findings are the only ones I'm obligated to go by." He pointed to the door. "I'm sorry for your loss, Amelia, but your grandmother died of natural causes. Take your little reporter friend and go find someone else to bother." He strutted into his office and slammed the door.

"Little reporter friend?" Nancy mimicked. "How do you think he'd like an exposé on who his biggest campaign contributors were in the last election and how much they dumped into it to get his fat ass elected?"

Amelia heard a woman laugh and turned her head. Terry Robles one of the few Hispanics in Briarton and the only one in the sheriff's department grinned up at her with her big dark eyes. "I'll give you three guesses on that one and the first two don't count."

"Sizemore and Hodges?" Nancy said with a sneer.

Officer Robles smiled. "You got it on the first try."

"How are you, Terry?" Amelia asked.

"Fed up with this bullshit job."

"Can't be easy with that fat asshole for a boss," Nancy said.

"Or my fellow officers who'll only give me back up if I give them head."

"Is that so?" Nancy said with interest and tapped her pad with her pen. "I think you and I should talk, Officer Robles."

"After we get things straight with Amelia and her grandmother," Terry said, glancing at the sheriff's door.

"Get what things straight, Terry?"

Terry Robles and her family had lived down the street from Amelia when they were kids and they'd ridden the bus together to school. Terry was a few years younger than Amelia, but they'd always been friendly. "When you first came in here about your grandmother, I went down to Rolling Acres and investigated her room."

"Did you find fingerprints on the headboard where someone might have been holding himself up?" Amelia imitated someone sitting astraddle someone on a bed and holding onto the headboard of a bed.

"I dusted and found plenty of fingerprints," the female officer said with a hand in her wavy black hair, "but that jackass in there wouldn't let me run them. He said it was a waste of taxpayers' money and your grandmother had died of a heart attack in her sleep."

"How about DNA?" Amelia asked. "Maybe on the wall next to the bed?"

Terry's dark eyes went wide, and she nodded. "A big biological sample."

"But fat ass in there wouldn't let you test it," Amelia said, glancing at the sheriff's door again with her anger rising.

"Said your grandma probably coughed it up while she was having her heart attack."

"Any way you can run the prints and the DNA without the sheriff knowing about it?" Nancy asked

Terry shook her head. "Sorry, Amelia. This is a small department with a tight budget. I could run the prints easy enough but without an exemplar I wouldn't know who to compare them to."

Amelia grinned. "Run the prints on the down low, Terry. I'd almost put money on it that they're in the system somewhere even if it's for a business license or something like that."

"I still can't help you with the DNA. That testing is

very expensive, and the sample can't be sent to the lab without the sheriff's express authorization."

Amelia took a deep breath and ran a hand through her thick red hair. "If you get a hit on the prints," she said, "I'll make certain we get a DNA test even if I have to pay for it myself."

"If the sample goes outside our chain of custody," Terry said glancing around the office, "it would probably be inadmissible in court, Amelia."

"We'll cross that bridge when we come to it, Terry. At this point, I'm just happy to hear you even have the damned sample."

Terry smiled. "Your grandmother was a sweet woman, Amelia," she said. "I'm a cop because of Miss O'Connor."

"Really?" Amelia said with her eyes wide.

"Remember how I used to come over on Sunday nights and watch Murder, She Wrote with you and your grandma?"

"Yah." Amelia vaguely remembered Terry being at their house on a few Sunday evenings, but she and Nathan always had friends in and out of the house.

"Miss O'Connor told me I had a detective's mind for solving those mysteries and said I should study and become a cop someday." She smiled. "And I did."

"Isn't that cool, Amelia," Nancy said with a wink. "I bet your grandmother would have liked to have known that."

Amelia nodded. "Yah, I bet she would."

"I wanted to go to her funeral," Terry said, "but I had to work."

"That's all right," Amelia told the officer. "It was a very small affair. You should come by the store sometime. Grandma is everywhere there."

"Really?" Terry said with a tweezered brow raised in confusion.

"Nathan and I put a little of her in everything we make. She was such a big part of our lives and we loved her so much."

Terry smiled. "I've been meaning to stop in. My husband and I just bought a house and I heard you have the cutest furniture and stuff."

"Please stop in and I'll make sure you get a good price on everything."

"Do you have any baby furniture?" Terry put a hand to her abdomen. "I might be needing some of that soon."

"Not yet," Nancy said with an uneasy grin, "but I think Nathan is working on some ideas."

"Cool," the officer said with a bright smile. "I'll stop in soon."

Cool, indeed. Amelia needed to have a talk with her brother about merchandising in the very near future. It sounded like Barnwood Builders needed to add cradles, cribs, and changing tables to their line along with picnic tables and lawn furniture.

———

NATHAN SAT beside Nancy as she held the little plastic wand from the pregnancy test kit in her shaking hand.

"Does it say anything yet?" he asked in an excited tone.

"It takes a few minutes, Nathan. Just calm down." Nancy reached out and took his hand.

"How many periods have you missed?" he asked again and took a sip from his second Budweiser for the evening.

"Two I think," Nancy said. "I'm really sorry, Nathan. I don't know how this could have happened. I've been on the pill for years." She glanced down at the wand and caught her breath as her blue eyes went wide.

"What?" he said, craning his neck to get a look at the wand.

"It's positive," Nancy whispered, staring up at Nathan. "I'm pregnant."

Nathan's face blossomed into a smile and he wrapped his muscular arms around Nancy. "We're pregnant," he amended joyfully. "We're going to have a baby."

"You're not upset?"

"Upset?" he gasped with a deep furrow in his brow. "How could I be upset? The woman I've fallen in love with is going to have my baby." He took her face into his hands and kissed her. "I'm the happiest man on Earth right now." When Nancy didn't speak, he asked. "Are you upset? Do you not want to have a baby—my baby?"

"Her eyes darted around her small studio apartment. "It's just not something I was expecting in my life right now," she said with her hand in her hair. "I live in one room and you live at home with your parents."

Nancy slapped her hand to her head and fell back on the bed. "Our parents are going to have shit fits over this."

"Our parents will get used to it, babe." He kissed her again. "We'll start looking for a bigger place right away—one with two or three bedrooms and a big kitchen."

"Maybe I can get Amelia to teach me to cook. My

mom is all thumbs in the kitchen unless you count dialing the phone to order delivery."

"Amelia's pretty good at that too," he said with a grin.

Nathan put his hand on Nancy's abdomen and smiled. "Amelia is going to be thrilled to be an aunt and I know she'll love to teach you her recipes."

"We're gonna need three bedrooms," she said, "because I'm gonna need an office. I'm just getting my career started, Nathan, and I don't intend to give it up just because I'm having a baby."

Nathan's blue eyes went wide. "I wouldn't expect you to, Nancy. I know you've put a lot of work into getting to where you are now, and I wouldn't think of asking you to stop."

"You mean even with me putting all our asses in hot water with this story?"

"Hey," he said, staring into her eyes. "You wrote the truth and if those bastards drag us into court for that, they're the ones who'll lose, not us."

Nancy smiled. "May I record that to play back to your sister?"

Nathan's brow pinched in confusion.

"You were pretty hard on Amelia and blamed her for the lawsuit."

"I already apologized for being an ass," he said and kissed Nancy again. "Do you want to get married?"

"Well, of course, I want to get married," she said, "but I'd always hoped for a little more romantic proposal."

"Do you want a big wedding with a three-tiered cake or can we run off to Vegas and have cupcakes on Fremont Street?"

"Cupcakes sound great right now," she said. "I'm starving."

Nathan bent and kissed her. "I love you, Nancy Adams."

"And I love you, Nathan Ryan," Nancy said with her soft hand on his stubbled cheek.

12

NANCY AND AMELIA SAT IN THE KITCHEN WAITING FOR Nathan to arrive with the copies of the Sunday Briarton Daily.

"I'm so nervous I think I'm going to puke," Nancy said before bolting to the bathroom.

Amelia grinned as she watched the girl run with her hand clapped over her mouth. She felt the hairs raise on her arms and glanced up to see the blue glow of her grandmother's Life Shadow appear in the chair beside her at the kitchen table.

"I think we should clue that girl in on what's going on," Jenny said into her ear with a giggle.

"I'm pretty certain she'll figure it out on her own soon enough, Grandma."

"Figure what out?" Nathan said as he walked in with his arms loaded with papers. "Who are you talking to?"

"Just chatting with Grandma." Amelia said.

Nathan's eyes flashed from empty chair to empty chair. "Is she here?"

"I'm right here, Nathan," Jenny yelled, causing an electrical shiver to run up Amelia's spine. The apparition waved her hands over her head comically to get her grandson's attention.

"She says hi, Bub," Amelia said with a grin and nodded to the chair where her grandmother sat waving. She studied her brother. "You don't see or feel anything?"

Nathan dropped the papers on the table and rubbed at his bare arms. "Maybe a shiver like a cat walked over my grave or something."

"Well, it's about damned time," the apparition of the old woman howled with delight. "I knew that Killian blood would rise in him sooner or later."

"What about Killian blood?" Nancy asked, wiping her mouth as she came from the bathroom.

Nathan turned. "You look pale, sweetheart." He took Nancy into his arms and kissed her sweaty forehead. "Are you all right?"

"Just nervous to see the story," she said and glanced at the table to see the stack of newspapers. She broke away from Nathan and grabbed a copy. "Oh, my god," she gasped and dropped into a chair.

"Yep," Nathan said with his face beaming, "you made the front page."

Amelia took one of the papers and unfolded it to see the headline: Briarton Pillars Suspected in Seventy-Year Old Murder. There was a photo of Margaret Adkins from the yearbook as well as the photos of Sizemore and Hodges from the same book.

"I think it was good to use those old yearbook photos, Nancy," Amelia said, "so people get a good idea about the ages of the people involved in this crime at the time it was committed. They were two kids who did horrible things to another kid."

"And went on to live unpunished for over half a century," Nathan added.

Amelia with her grandmother's Life Shadow standing over her shoulder read the article from beginning to end. Nancy had done a wonderful job of laying out the story from the arrival of the students at Lake Hamilton, the witness statements telling how people saw Margaret leave with Sizemore and how Hodges followed them soon after.

She capped the story with the group photo of the kids leaving, noting Sizemore was missing his fancy belt and Margaret was missing all together. The final photo was one of Nathan in the barn holding up the belt he'd taken from beside the bones of Margaret Adkins and one of the coroner leading a man carrying a nearly weightless body bag filled with Margaret's bones.

She made no accusations, leaving that to the readers to decide.

"Now that girl knows how to write a newspaper story," Jenny whispered into Amelia's ear.

"Grandma likes your article, Nancy."

Nancy looked up from her copy of the paper and smiled. "I have a follow up planned with all the evidence Terry Robles found in her room at Rolling Acres. I'm just waiting for the DNA results to come back."

Roy Tate wouldn't authorize DNA testing on the biological sample Terry had collected at Rolling Acres, but Robert Kusak, when he heard about it, made all the arrangements for the sample to be transported to the Chicago lab and agreed to pay for the testing. Terry signed it out of evidence at the sheriff's office and flew with it to Chicago until she put it into the hands of the attendant at the testing facility. There would be no problems with chain of custody for the sample and when it proved to be David Sizemore's, it would seal his fate for a modern case of murder.

Nancy's phone rang. "This is either good news from Kusak or the shit's hit the fan," she said as she swiped the screen to answer.

After speaking for only a few minutes, Nancy disconnected with a bright smile on her face. "We need to get to Rolling Acres," she gasped. "The DNA came in on the belt. It was saturated with Margaret's because it had lain there with her decomposing body, but," she added, "they found Sizemore's on it too and with all the photographic evidence, the DA is formally charging the bastard with Margaret Adkins' murder." She put her hand to her abdomen. "I'm gonna puke again," she gasped before slapping a hand to her mouth and rushing to the bathroom.

"I'll be glad when all of this is over with," Nathan said as he watched Nancy, "so her stomach will finally settle down."

Amelia grinned up at her brother. "Bub, I think this is only the beginning of things for you."

They rushed into Amelia's car and drove to Rolling Acres where they found the parking lot filled with police vehicles and reporters with their cameras flashing as elderly David Sizemore, handcuffed and escorted by his lawyer was rolled in a wheelchair by Officer Terry Robles to a waiting squad car for transport to the sheriff's office.

Nancy got out and snapped a few pictures. "I can't believe this," she said as they watched Sizemore being driven away.

"It's all because of you, sweetheart," Nathan said,

giving Nancy a big hug. "That poor girl is finally going to get her day in court because of your hard work." Nancy grinned at him with her phone at her ear.

"We still have to get Grandma her day in court," Amelia said with a sad smile.

"That was Kusak," Nancy said. "He wants me at the office ASAP to do a follow up on Sizemore's arrest and that piece on Jenny." She grinned at Amelia. "And you if it's all right to spill the family secrets."

Amelia shrugged. "It's your story, Nancy. You can write whatever you want about me. I know you'll have my back and trust you completely."

"That's great, Babe," Nathan said as they all piled back into Amelia's car. "It looks like you finally hit the big time with this one." He glanced at his sister. "Go easy on the family angle, though. We don't want to give my mom a stroke just yet."

"Speak for yourself, Bubba," Amelia muttered. "Is the old man finally going to give you a desk?" Amelia asked, looking at Nancy in the rearview mirror.

"With all the work he just piled on me," she said with a long sigh, "he's gonna have to give me a damned cot."

"Don't let him take advantage of you, Nancy." Nathan squeezed her hand. "We need to have time to look at apartments."

"You two have something to tell me?" Amelia asked with a grin.

"Nancy and I have decided to move in together," Nathan said.

"Is that all?" she persisted.

"We're looking for a nice big one with two bedrooms or three, so I can have an office," Nancy said, and Amelia could see the smile on her freckled face.

"That's great," she said. "I bet Mom and Dad will be thrilled."

Nathan's eyes went wide. "I haven't told them yet, sis, so don't blow our surprise."

"No worries there, Bub. Mom still isn't speaking to me and I seldom see Dad unless it's in passing at Home Depot."

"We should just go ahead and tell her, Nathan," Nancy said from the back seat. "She's not stupid and will figure it out soon enough."

Amelia smiled. "I'm guessing it's going to be due in early February."

She watched her brother's mouth fall open. "It really sucks having a psychic for a sister."

"How long have you known?" Nancy asked with her head on Nathan's shoulder.

"Grandma told me a few weeks ago."

Nathan's head fell back on the seat and he groaned. "We're doomed. We'll never have any secrets in this damned family." He glanced up at Amelia grinning in the mirror. "Did she happen to tell you if we're expecting a girl or a boy?"

"She did say to expect one with a strong gift."

Nathan groaned louder.

"And the gift usually comes in girls?" Nancy asked enthusiastically.

"According to Grandma," Amelia said with a grin.

"Then I guess we'd better start picking out girl names," Nathan said with a sigh.

"When is the wedding?" Amelia asked.

"Didn't Grandma tell you that too?" Nathan said in a gruff tone.

"Nathan," Nancy scolded, "don't be rude."

"I'm sorry, Sis. It's been a long, tough go of it."

Amelia raised a brow. "And you don't think it's been the same for me?"

"We're going to fly to Vegas next week," Nancy cut in, "get married in one of those drive-thru chapels by an Elvis impersonator, and then go eat cupcakes on Fremont Street."

"That sounds cool," Amelia muttered as she drove toward the square. "Mom's gonna love it."

Amelia heard her brother groan again and saw his head fall back on the seat.

They dropped Nancy at the Daily office and then returned to the store. Nathan went to his workshop and Amelia opened for business. The Sunday hours were from one to five and she made it with minutes to spare.

Two women stood at the door when Amelia opened. Both were in their forties and were dressed in black. She didn't find that odd, but their green and lavender hair was a bit off-putting.

Their T-shirts read: Macabre Creations with white skull and cross bones on the pocket over their left breasts. They walked into the store and began picking up pieces and reading the notes on the backs with interest.

"What we're really looking for," one of them said as she returned a plaque to the wall, "are pieces from that murder barn. Where are they?"

The statement took Amelia by surprise, but she didn't know why. She'd been fielding phone calls all week from people looking for such items. What shocked her was coming face to face with some of those people.

"We've only just taken that barn down," Amelia said in reply, repeating what she'd been telling people over the phone, "and haven't had much time to put anything together yet."

One of the women slipped a silver business card case from the back pocket of her jeans and opened it to hand Amelia a business card. "Well, when you do, give me a call. We'd be interested to see what you come up with for the inventory in our shop." She smiled as she picked up one of Amelia's wooden boxes. "We specialize a little more in creep than cute," she said, "but some boxes like this with silver skull hardware might work as long as they're made from wood that came out of that barn where they found the remains of that girl's body."

"And we'd pay a premium price if the wood had actually touched the body in some way," the other woman added as she studied the price tag on the box she held. "Say three times your list price here."

Amelia rolled her eyes as she added the card to a pile beside the cash register. "I'll keep that in mind," she said as she watched the women wander through the store. Where did these people come from? Amelia knew there was a huge market online for murder and serial killer memorabilia, but she never thought she or her store would become part of that craziness.

Amelia picked up the box the woman had handled. Did she want her things to be amongst the women's collection of macabre creations?

The door opened, and a petite blonde walked in. She had a familiar look, but Amelia couldn't place her. "May I help you?"

The woman approached with a sad smile on her face. "Amelia?" She offered her hand. "It's Connie," she said, "Connie Miller. We were in Mrs. Hastings' English class together."

"Of course," Amelia said, taking the woman's hand. "How are you? It's been a while since sophomore English."

Connie Miller, like Amelia, hadn't been in the popular crowd at Briarton High. They'd both spent time in quiet corners in the library. While Amelia's notoriety had come from having a crazy grandmother, Connie's had come from having a murdered mother during her freshman year and a brother who was accused of the killing and convicted. High School for Connie had been particularly unbearable.

"This is a nice place, Amelia," Connie said, glancing around at the barn wood plaques on the walls and the furniture displays. "I'm glad to see you've done well for yourself."

"Thanks," Amelia said with an uneasy smile, sensing the woman had more on her mind than wall art. "And how about you, Connie? How are you?"

Connie coughed to clear her throat. "I'm friends with a woman at the paper and she told me that another woman who works there is writing a story about you and your grandma." Her eyes darted around the store. "I was sorry to hear about her passing, by the way."

"Thanks, Connie." Amelia motioned to the display futon. "Why don't we sit while you tell me why you're really here today."

Connie adjusted the strap of her purse over her shoulder and sat. "Am I that obvious?" she asked with a nervous smile.

Amelia sat beside the woman. "What can I do for you Connie?"

The woman cleared her throat again. "You remember what happened to my mom, right?"

Amelia nodded.

"Well, they convicted my brother Bobby for killing her, but I never believed he did it. Bobby and Mom had some knock-down-drag-out fights," she said, "but he loved her and would never have hurt her like that."

If Amelia remembered correctly, Barbara Miller had been found with her throat cut, her eyes gouged out, and her tongue cut out. It had been a bloody and brutal murder, and her son Bobby had found his mother's body, gotten bloody holding her, and then had been accused and convicted of the murder.

"What do you want me to do, Connie?" Amelia asked as she handed the woman a paper towel to wipe the tears running down her face.

"My friend at the paper said Nancy told her you and your grandmother are mediums like that woman on television who goes to houses and talks to the dead."

"I don't know that it's exactly like that," Amelia muttered.

"If you went to my house could you see who really killed my mom, Amelia?"

Amelia's mouth fell open. "I don't know, Connie. It depends on a lot of different things."

"Like what?"

How did she put this without sounding like a complete nutjob? "Well," Amelia said with a deep sigh, "it would depend on whether or not your mom is still there to show me what happened to her."

Amelia had never considered Connie might still be living in the house her mother had been killed in. She'd gone to stay with her grandparents after the murder and during her brother's trial.

Connie wiped her eyes and blew her nose. "I don't

know if she is or not," she finally said, shaking her blonde head. "I used to think she was still there, but it's been a long time now, and I don't know." She took Amelia's hand. "Would you come over to my house and see? My brother has a new attorney and he's trying to get him a new trial." Tears washed down her face again. "They need new evidence, Amelia. If you could come and see what really happened to my mom, maybe we could get Bobbie out of prison."

Amelia rested a hand atop Connie's. "I'll come over, Connie, but—"

"But?" the woman asked, wiping her eyes with the soggy paper towel.

"But what if your mother shows me your brother killing her?"

"Then I suppose I'll have to accept that he did it after all," Connie said. "When can you come over?"

"Let me check my calendar, Connie, and I'll give you a call next week if you'll leave me your number."

Connie surprised Amelia by throwing her arms around her neck. "Thank you so much, Amelia. You have no idea how much this means to me." She took a business card from her purse and handed it to Amelia. "My home number and address are on there and I look forward to hearing from you soon."

Amelia studied the card. Constance Miller, CPA, her address, and phone number. "You're an accountant?"

Connie nodded. "Went to college at State and have been in business from the house for almost twenty years now."

"Barnwood Builders is going to need one come tax time," Amelia said with a smile.

"You probably need one now," the woman said in

reply. "When you come by, why don't you bring along what records you have, and I can get things started for you."

"That sounds great," Amelia said. "I'll check my schedule and give you a call to set things up."

Connie offered her hand. "Thanks again, Amelia. I really appreciate it."

Amelia took the woman's hand and received a slight electrical charge that caused Amelia to stare around the room, looking for the familiar glow of a Life Shadow but she didn't see one. "You have no idea how much I'll appreciate having someone else to deal with Nathan's horrid bookkeeping system." Her eyes continued to dart around the store.

Connie grinned. "Sounds like a fair trade to me. You help me with my brother, and I'll help you with yours."

Connie dropped Amelia's hand and left the store. Amelia's eyes followed the woman out onto the side-walk, searching for the blue glow of a Life Shadow. She supposed it was possible Connie's mother had at-tached herself to the woman in some way. She was going to need to study Jenny's notebooks a little closer.

13

———

TERRY ROBLES TOOK THE DINNER TRAY TO THE CELL holding David Sizemore.

The old man glanced up from his paperback and grinned. "Well, if it isn't the little Mex come to bring an old man his supper. Did Roy make you cook it too?" he asked as he put the book aside. "I like Mexican." He patted the bunk. "Why don't you come on in here and give me a little."

Terry slid the tray onto the shelf in his cell door. "It's fried chicken from the kitchen here in the jail," she said, "and my family is from Ecuador not Mexico."

Sizemore shuffled in his inmate slippers from his bunk to the door to collect the tray. He looked at the food and smiled. "Looks better than that shit I used to get at Rolling Acres."

Terry shook her head. "I bet this is sure a comedown after being in a nice place like that."

He shrugged his stooped shoulders. "From one prison to another," he mumbled. "My dear daughter, Lilly said it's where I belong." He began to chuckle as he sat down with the tray of food on his lap. "If the little bitch only knew the half of it."

"The half of what, Mr. Sizemore?" Terry asked as she leaned against the bars of Sizemore's private cell in the jail. Roy Tate had arranged for the old man to be housed away from the general population of the county jail for his own safety and for Sizemore's comfort.

He'd made the old man Terry's responsibility and while the female deputy resented him for it, she thought she might take it as an opportunity as well. Sizemore was a bragger and Terry recognized the type. If she could get him talking, maybe she could help Amelia's case and get justice for Miss O'Connor.

"Why don't you show me those pretty brown, Mex titties?" Sizemore teased as he tore chicken from the bone with his teeth.

"Why don't you tell me what it is your daughter doesn't know the half of, Mr. Sizemore."

He smiled as he chewed. "That stuck up little white bread cunt would run to China with that pencil-dick husband of hers if she knew what her daddy had really been up to all these years." He chuckled. "She thinks she knows," he shook his balding head, "but she doesn't know shit."

Terry stood with her breasts protruding between the bars. "So, tell me, Mr. Sizemore, and I'll make sure she finds out." She lifted her mini-tape recorder for Sizemore to see. She used it during their conversations and the old man was accustomed to seeing it.

David Sizemore ran his tongue over the bone of the chicken leg. "Leggy Peggy may have been my first," he said with a chuckle, "and that dried up old Irish cunt, my last," he tossed the bone onto the tray, "but there was a whole hell of a lot more in between."

Terry's heart began to pound as she clicked on the

recorder in her uniform pocket. "How many, Mr. Sizemore? How many other women besides Peggy Adkins and Jennifer O'Connor did you kill?"

Sizemore shoveled mashed potatoes and corn into his mouth while he considered Terry's question. She could almost see the wheels turning behind his watery blue eyes. "Killed me a Mex down in Tijuana with my Daddy once," he said with a grin. "My Daddy's the one who showed me what fun it is to get my rocks off that way."

"Your father murdered women too?"

"Not women," Sizemore spat, "just the hired house-sluts and whores from West-town or brothels we visited when traveling."

Terry's hands began to tremble. "How many women have you killed Mr. Sizemore?"

"Like I said they weren't all real women. Some were just hired help from the menial classes and others like Leggy Peggy where nothing but whores who were going to end up dead from rotted pussy anyhow." He shrugged. "My wife Melody was a real woman and I hated to have to end her, but she caught me in the basement with the gardener's wife and threw a fit."

"I thought I read that Mrs. Sizemore committed suicide," Terry said with trembling lips.

Melody Sizemore had been found by her daughter Marie hanging in her husband's office of an apparent suicide in 1969. Two years later Marie was found hanging in the same place.

Sizemore grinned and ran a greasy finger over his throat. "Rope burns cover a lot."

"And your daughter" Terry ventured. "Did you kill her too?"

Sizemore's face took on a look of disgust. "Marie was my daughter," he hissed. "I'm not one of those low-class daughter-diddlers. Marie never got over losing her mother and killed herself. Lilly told me, when she put me in Rolling Acres, that Marie always suspected I'd killed Melody and staged her suicide. She killed herself where she did to let me know she knew." He smiled. "Had Marie been a son, I'd have shown him the pleasures of wringing the life from a cunt while he blew his load in her ass the way my Daddy showed me, but Melody could never seem to push anything but sniveling girls out of her pussy, so I was denied that simple pleasure and Lilly has never given me a grandson." He shrugged. "I suppose the Sizemore legacy ends with me."

"What did you do with the bodies?" Terry asked boldly.

Sizemore shuffled back and put his empty tray on the rack. "Have you ever seen the rose garden on my estate, young lady?" He winked at Terry. "Nice roses are all in the fertilizer."

Terry Robles took the empty tray to the kitchen and then returned to her desk where she made a copy of the recording of David Sizemore's conversation. She then followed the chain of command and took the recorder into Roy Tate's office where she played it for the sheriff.

"Give me that thing," Tate said, and grabbed the recorder from Terry's hand. "I suppose you think this is gonna push you up in the department or something?"

"No, sir," she said, knowing it would get her no place in Tate's department. "I thought it was something you should be aware of. Sizemore—and his father according to his own words—are fucking serial killers."

The sheriff made a sputtering sound and slammed a fist on his desk. "Now you're starting to sound like that crazy Ryan or O'Connor or whatever the hell she's calling herself these days. You both need to keep your damned female noses where they belong."

Terry slipped her hand into the pocket of her uniform trousers and flipped on the other small recorder she carried there. She would add this tape to her collection of others where the sheriff and her fellow officers degraded her or demanded sexual favors from her if she requested their assistance.

"And just where do we belong, Sheriff Tate?" Terry asked with a raised brow.

"Well, for starters," the sheriff said with a grin, "you could get down here between my legs and suck my cock. It's the only place a woman on this force really belongs and if you expect to stay here, you'd better start showing me a little gratitude that way."

"My husband doesn't like sharing his toys, sheriff," Terry said.

"Then maybe your husband should be paying your damned salary rather than me."

Terry stood. She'd heard enough from Sheriff Roy Tate to know he wouldn't do anything with the tape of Sizemore's astounding confession.

"Oh, don't run off mad Officer Robles. Why don't you come bend over my desk and let me slide in for a pump or two? I'm sure you'll enjoy it. Maggie and Syl get their rocks off every time I throw a good hump into 'em." He grinned. "They're both real screamers."

Maggie Herman and Sylvia Reynolds were the two office assistants who did filing, and Terry had no doubt the women bent over the sheriff's desk and got on their knees between his legs regularly to keep their county jobs in Roy Tate's office.

"They're both real fakers, sheriff," Terry said before turning and walking out the door.

———

NANCY LISTENED to the recording of Sizemore's conversation with her mouth open and her eyes wide.

"And what did the sheriff say about it?" Amelia asked with her trembling hands tight around her coffee cup. "That sonofabitch just admitted killing my grandmother."

"He took my recorder and then asked for a blow job because the only place a woman on the force belongs is on her knees between his legs."

"He actually said that?" Nancy gasped in shock.

Terry took out a small tape, replaced the one of Sizemore's confession, and played the conversation between herself and Sheriff Tate.

"I can't believe that bastard," Amelia spat. "What are we going to do with this now?"

Terry smiled. "I took it directly across the street to the DA's office and played it for him."

"And was his response any different than the sheriff's?" Amelia asked without much hope. Law enforcement in the county had been in the pockets of the Sizemores for as long as Amelia could remember.

"As we speak there are deputies with shovels at the Sizemore Estate, digging up the damned rose garden." Terry grinned as she showed them the copies of the warrants. "I'm gonna frame these damned things."

Terry's cell phone rang. After a short conversation

she turned to Nancy. "You should get over there if you want the scoop of a lifetime, Nancy. That was Franny from the DA's office and they're starting to uncover bodies."

Nancy jumped to her feet. "Oh, my God," she gasped and grabbed for her notebook. She scooped up the tapes Terry had given her and dropped them into her bag. "Tate is fucking finished in Briarton," she spat as she rushed toward the door.

Amelia was about to follow when Terry grabbed her wrist. "That's not all, Amelia."

"What?" Amelia asked in a rush to follow Nancy to the Sizemore Estate.

"Franny also said they got the DNA results back from the lab in Chicago."

Amelia slid back into her chair. "And?"

"It was Sizemore's," Terry confirmed with a broad smile. "They're pressing charges for your grandmother's murder as we speak." She reached over and squeezed Amelia's hand. "The DNA along with the fingerprints on the bed, and Sizemore's damned confession on that tape will make certain that old man takes his last breath in a maximum-security facility wearing an orange jumpsuit and black rubber flip-flops."

Amelia threw her arms around Terry's neck. "Thank you so much, Terry. Grandma was right. You've got what it takes to be a detective."

Terry batted back tears. "I wish she was still here to tell me herself, Amelia."

Terry shivered and brushed at her arms as the tiny hairs rose on them and she saw Amelia staring over her shoulder and smiling. "Grandma knows, Terry and I'm sure she couldn't be happier."

She turned for a quick glance behind her, but Terry didn't see anything but Amelia's kitchen. "Shall we join Nancy and the rest of my cohorts from the department to watch them unearth the final nails in Sizemore and Tate's coffins?"

Amelia smiled. "That sounds great to me. But why Sizemore and Tate?"

Terry grinned. "After listening to what Tate had to say, the DA contacted the City Council and they're relieving the sheriff of his command."

"Where does that leave you, Terry?"

"Pat Armstrong is next in line for command," she said, "but he just put in his papers for retirement and the rest of those bastards are under investigation."

"So?"

Terry grinned. "I'm taking the Sergeant's exam next week through the State Police Board and if I pass, they're putting my name forward as acting sheriff until the elections next spring."

"That's great, Terry," Amelia said, giving the woman another hug. "Grandma would be so damned proud."

"Come on," the female officer said, "I want to get over to the Sizemore Estate and see what they've found under those damned rose bushes."

"More Margaret Adkins I'd imagine," Amelia said sadly.

"And that sonofabitch never even considered them human beings," Terry said, shaking her head. "He called them hired help and whores."

"Do you think a jury will ever hear it?"

"Probably not," Terry said with a sigh. "A good attorney would get it thrown out because I didn't tell him I was recording that particular conversation and get his OK."

"But you had his approval to record others?"

Terry nodded. "In writing with his shaky old signature on the dotted line."

"Maybe the old bastard will plead out when his attorney sees all the evidence you have against him." Amelia locked the door behind them and walked to their cars parked in spaces in front of Barnwood Builders.

"We can only hope," Terry said. "Did you see the Out of Business sign on Briarton Home Furnishings?"

Amelia grinned. "One down and one to go."

Nathan parked his red pickup beside Amelia's car and rolled down the window.

"What the hell's going on, sis? I've been trying to call Nancy and her phone keeps going to voicemail."

Amelia waved at Terry who got in her personal vehicle and backed out. "All hell's broken loose with Sizemore, Bub. Nancy's over at his place where they're digging up his famous rose garden in search of bodies."

"Bodies?" Nathan gasped. "What bodies?"

Amelia walked over and opened the passenger door to climb in. "Sizemore's a damned serial killer," she said as she pushed food wrappers from Burger King and Taco Bell as well as empty soda cups into the floor to make room in the seat. "He confessed to Terry Robles and now the whole police department is over there digging the place up."

"Along with my pregnant fiancé?" he griped as he backed out as well.

"It's her scoop," Amelia said with a grin, "and it will likely go viral if it's as big as Terry thinks it is."

Nathan shook his head. "The Adkins girl, Grandma Jen, and other women too?"

"They have him for Grandma too," Amelia said. "The DNA from her wall came back and it was a positive match to Sizemore. They busted him, and Terry says the bastard will never see the light of day as a free man again."

Nathan reached over and took Amelia's hand. "I bet you were glad to hear that."

"We all were, Bubba. We all were."

"I wish I could have been there to see Sizemore's face when they told him," Nathan said.

"I bet he still can't believe he's in jail for killing a commoner like Jenny O'Connor," Amelia hissed.

14

———————

David Sizemore woke with a heaviness on his chest and gasped for breath, suspecting another heart attack. He suspected it was time. He'd had a good run and with these new charges, he'd never get to go home again.

His eyes flew open in the darkness of his jail cell and it took him a minute to orientate himself. He wasn't at home anymore. He wasn't even in that hideous Rolling Acres with Mamie fussing over him. He was in Roy Tate's damned jail.

Sizemore tried to sit up but the weight on his chest kept him down. In the glow of the light coming through the barred window of the door, he saw the form of a woman. He blinked to clear his vision and gasped when he recognized the pretty face of Leggy Peggy Adkins staring down at him.

"What the hell are you doing here, Peggy?" he demanded. "You're dead."

"We're here to make certain you get what's coming to you, David," Peggy said in her sweet childish voice that had never fit with her woman's shapely body.

"We? he gasped, struggling for breath. "Who else is here?"

The wrinkled face of Jenny O'Connor smiled down at him from over Peggy's naked shoulder. "I thought I'd tag along and help Peggy out, David."

"Help her what, you wrinkled old Irish witch?" he gasped and coughed.

Jenny wore a nightgown, but for the first time, David realized Peggy was as naked as she'd been when he'd sealed her in the floor of that old barn. She sat on his chest with her long legs spread and he smiled at the sight of what glistened between her firm, shapely thighs.

"Bring that on closer, girl, so I can have a good smell of that sweet pussy if it's going to be the last thing on this Earth I'm ever going to smell."

"If that's what you really want, David," she said and bounced closer to his head.

David Sizemore coughed with each jarring movement over his congested chest as he took a deep breath in order to get a whiff of the girl's sweet musk. "What a way for a man to go," he said as he opened his mouth and stuck out his tongue, trying to get a taste.

"Did you enjoy what you did to us, David?" Peggy asked.

"Huh?" he asked in surprise. "Yah, sure, I enjoyed it. It's what women are for—to be enjoyed by men. I didn't enjoy the old cunt as much, but I enjoyed you very much, Peggy."

Peggy's smile turned dark. "Then I'm going to enjoy this," she said. "Look what you did to me, David," Peggy yelled and grasped the sides of the man's head to force him to look up at her face. "Look what you and Keith did to me." To the side of the cot,

David saw a flicker of blue light and wondered for a minute if a television was on. His eyes darted from Peggy to the blue light and he was shocked to see the form of Keith Hodges materialize to stare down at him with his accusing eyes.

As David Sizemore stared up, the once pretty young face of Peggy Adkins began to swell and turn dark. The aroma of her sweet musk turned to one of putrefaction and horror filled David Sizemore as he watched flies begin to swarm over Peggy's big, brown eyes. The flies left and were replaced with fat, white maggots crawling over her discolored eyeballs. He opened his mouth to scream and the maggots fell to squirm over his tongue.

"This is what you did to me, David." Peggy said with a horrific chuckle.

David spat and shook his head to get the maggots out of his mouth, but more fell from Peggy's eyes until there were no eyeballs left. Putrid viscera wept from the sockets and fell into his face. The stench of rotting flesh filled his nostrils and he gagged, choking on the bile rising up from his stomach.

"Stop," David groaned. He thrashed on the narrow cot as Peggy tightened her thighs around his thrashing head. Her face had swollen into a mass of green and black tissue as had her once shapely body. The skin on her breasts blackened and cracked as green slime oozed from her nipples.

"Suck on these now, David," she told him in a voice that didn't come from Peggy's leering, lipless mouth. The disgusting slime dripped into his mouth. Sizemore tightened his lips and the foul filth ran into his nose.

As David Sizemore watched in horror, the body of

Peggy Adkins putrefied before his eyes and began to slide off her bones. He screamed and gasped for breath. Every time he screamed or tried to suck in air the foulness that had been Peggy's body filled his mouth, nose, and lungs.

David Sizemore took his final gasping breath on a narrow cot in the basement of the county jail in Briarton, filling his county issued pink underwear with the foul excrement of his dying body.

"It's time to go now, Dave," Keith Hodges said, holding his hand out to his oldest friend.

Sizemore sat up, feeling unusually good. "Where are we going, Keith?"

The room suddenly shook, and the floor opened up. "What the hell?" Sizemore gasped as he studied the red haze in the pit below. "Must have been an earthquake that opened up the floor into an old coal mine," Sizemore ventured as he stared down into the pit.

Keith took his friend's hand. "It's time to go, Dave. They're waiting for us down there."

Peggy sat on the cot, but her body was clothed now in the skirt and sweater she'd worn to the picnic—the ones David had torn from her body in that horrible barn.

"I'm so sorry, Peggy," Keith said and reached out to touch her. "Can you ever forgive me for the part I played in your death?"

Peggy glanced up from the cot to study the form of the handsome boy she'd known in high school. Her brown eyes sparkled with her smile. "If I forgive you," she said, "you won't have to go down there with him."

"But we both deserve an eternity in darkness for what we did to you, Peggy," Keith said, reaching out to touch the girl's pretty face. "I'm so very, very sorry for what I did to you and I understand if you can't see fit to forgive me."

Peggy reached out and took the young man's hand. "I forgive you, Keith. I was bitter for a very long time, but that's over now, and I can find forgiveness in my heart for you. It's something I have to do, or I'll never be free of this either." She glared at Sizemore whose eyes had gone wide, staring down at the writhing mass of bodies in the pit below. "You don't have to spend eternity in darkness with that fool, Keith. Drop his hand and come with me into the light."

Sizemore held fast to the hand of his friend. "What are you two talking about, Keith?" He glared at the form of Peggy. "Keith is coming with me. Keith always comes with me. It's his place. It always will be, and he knows it."

"But I have to take him into the pit, Peggy. It's my penance for what I did to you at his behest."

Peggy Adkins smiled at the young man who'd helped to take her life all those years ago. "There are plenty of others to see him into the pit, Keith." She nodded to the edge of the floor where the grasping black hands of creatures from the pit reached for David Sizemore's orange-clad legs. "You've asked for forgiveness, Keith, and I've forgiven you." She extended her hand. "It's time for us to go into the light now." Peggy nodded to a glowing portal. "I've been waiting for a very long time to feel the peace in that light and I think you have too."

Keith's eyes went wide as he took Peggy's offered hand. "I'm allowed to go in there?"

The pretty girl smiled. "If your apology was sincere." She stepped into the bright portal with Keith following close behind.

"Keith," David Sizemore screamed as he watched his friend disappear into the light and clawed hands grasped his legs to tug him into the dark pit where he saw the glowing embers of long-dead fires and smelled the stink of sulfurous gas. "Don't leave me, Keith."

"Keith Hodges is gone, David," the form of Jenny O'Connor said with a smile on her face. The pretty face David remembered from school—not the wrinkled old face from Rolling Acres. By her side stood her boyfriend/husband Ned.

"Neither Peggy nor I have to think of you again, David," Jenny said, "but you're going to spend eternity in the dark remembering what it was like to choke to death the way you choked your victims."

"I always wondered what Hell looked like," Ned said with a grin as he watched David dangling from the edge of the concrete jail house floor. "And it does my soul good to be the one to send your hateful, murdering ass there." Ned stomped his work-booted foot on Sizemore's fingers until the man released his hold on this plane of existence and fell, screaming into the next one.

Sizemore screamed for mercy as he fell and watched the floor above him knit back together.

―――――

"It looks like a simple heart attack to me," the coroner said as he knelt over the dead body of David Sizemore.

"No autopsy then?" Sargent Terry Robles asked the

old man with a grin tugging at the corners of her mouth.

"Just a waste of the taxpayers' money," he said as he stood. "Sizemore suffered from congestive heart failure and had suffered three previous attacks." The old man shrugged his shoulders and pulled off his rubber gloves. "This one is easy-peasy, officer."

"It's detective sergeant now," Terry said, flashing the gold shield hooked on her belt.

"Of course, it is," the coroner said with an insincere smile. "Between you and Amelia Ryan, I'm sure you'll have all the cold cases taken care of in this department very soon."

Terry grinned. "We just took care of about sixty of them at Sizemore's. Didn't we? How are those autopsy identifications going?"

The old doctor rolled his eyes. "Since Sizemore admitted taking the lives of his house servants, I've been going through the missing persons reports over the past fifty years or so and flagging those with ties to Sizemore's Estate in any way, but it's going to take a while to get through them all."

"He mentioned prostitutes from West Town too," Terry said.

The coroner glanced down at Sizemore's body again and shook his head. "Who'd have thought we'd have one of the most prolific serial killers in the country right here in our midst, playing at being an upstanding citizen of this community."

"BTK was a deacon in his church," Terry said with a shrug of her uniformed shoulders. "Most of those guys fooled people like that, Doc."

"But this man was my friend," the doctor said with

a sigh as he stared at the still form of David Sizemore. "He fooled me and I'm a doctor."

"The only doctor he might not have fooled was a head-shrinker, and you're not one of those. Are you?"

"No, but I still should have seen something."

"David Sizemore was a serial killer and so was his father." Terry shrugged. "Maybe even his father's father. Killing women during their sex games was something the Sizemore men enjoyed and passed down from father to son, according to him." She nodded to the dead man on the bunk.

The doctor shook his gray head. "I wonder where all those other bodies are buried."

Terry grinned. "Maybe Amelia will come across them someday."

"Not soon, I hope," the doctor said. "My autopsy room already looks like the catacombs beneath Paris with all the unidentified remains stacked in there like cord wood."

"If you'd like me to help you go through those old missing persons files," she said, "I'd be happy to."

"That would certainly be helpful, Sargent," he said respectfully. "I'm looking for females fifteen to forty who had anything to do with the Sizemore Estate or Sizemore family and business." He took a breath. "I found one file for a Sizemore cousin who went missing in 1958 after a family get together and a woman who worked at the family business who disappeared in 1963 after a company Christmas party."

"Picking up women at picnics, parties, and big functions seemed to be his MO," Terry said with a sigh.

The doctor shook his head again. "I still can't believe nobody picked up on it in all those years.

Someone had to have seen the pattern. There's a Sizemore event and then a woman goes missing."

"The department records are all computerized now," Terry said. "I should be able to go into Missing Persons and narrow the search with things like female fifteen to forty, Sizemore, and missing after attending function of some sort."

The old doctor smiled. "That might speed things up some."

"I'll give it a shot, Doc, and then we can fall back on the paper files for particulars."

"You gotta love this digital age we live in," the old man said before taking his leave.

"Damn that old man stinks," Andy Powell said as he came strolling into the cell. "I'm glad you're cleaning him up, Robles and not me."

Terry turned with a smile on her face to one of the men who'd made her life hell on the job for years with his snide comments and crude talk. "Detective Sergeants don't clean up shit in the holding cells, Officer Powell. You do." Terry laughed as she pushed past the gaping officer. "I'm sure the funeral home will be here for him soon, but you should at least get him straightened up on the bunk and maybe change his shorts."

15

—————

Nathan planed down the boards of the platform
that had covered Margaret's body and found them to
be beautiful red oak.

"I'm glad you decided to do this," Amelia said as
they carried his project up the steps to Grace Adkins'
home.

"Seemed to be the least I could do," he said as
Amelia knocked on the door. "I didn't like the idea of
making things for that ghoulish Macabre Creations
outfit."

"Me neither, Bub, but they'll pay well."

Grace Adkins answered and when her old eyes
recognized Amelia, she flew to her and wrapped her
arms around her neck.

"We owe you so much, Miss Ryan," Grace said
with tears choking her voice. "You brought our Peggy
back to us when nobody else did."

The old woman had expressed the same senti-
ments at her sister's funeral, but Amelia still found it
difficult to respond without tears.

"Sizemore had her well-hidden the same as all his

other victims," Amelia whispered as she backed away from Grace.

"Who is it, Gracie?" Amelia heard her brother Tom call from the living room.

"It's Amelia Ryan," the old woman called back as she smiled up at Nathan. "She's here with her brother and they've brought us a gift."

"Well, bring 'em in," he yelled back, and Amelia heard him righting the recliner.

"Thomas' lung cancer has gone into remission since you brought Peggy home," Grace whispered. "His doctors don't know what to think about the change in him."

They followed Grace into the living room where Tom Adkins met them with his hand extended in greeting. He stared at Nathan with his mouth open.

"Damn if you don't look the spitting image of Ned O'Connor."

"My grandfather on my mother's side," Nathan said as he shook the old man's hand.

"Ned and I were friends," Tom said. "He spent days searching for Peggy with me back when it happened." He wiped a tear from his cheek. "Some would call it strange that it was his grandchildren who finally found her and brought her home to us after all this time."

"It was our pleasure, sir," Nathan said. "And I made this for your porch." He nodded to the gleaming red oak swing. "The wood came from the platform covering your sister's body and Amelia and I thought the two of you should have it in memory of her."

Grace ran a hand over the back of the swing with her eyes closed. "Now she's really home, Tommy," the old woman muttered with tears running down her wrinkled cheeks again. "I can feel her here now."

"It's a fine gift, young man," Tom said, staring at the swing and his sister. "Your grandfather would have been a proud man."

"That newspaper story," Grace finally said to Amelia, "said you could see and talk to Peggy. Was that true? Did you talk to my poor sister in that barn about what happened to her?"

Amelia took a deep breath. "My grandmother was born with the gift of being able to see and speak to the dead and passed that gift on to me," she said. "Yes, I saw and spoke with Peggy. It's how I knew she was there somewhere."

Amelia didn't want to relate the horrible details of their poor sister's death to these two. They'd been through enough.

"What did she say?" Tom asked. "Did she talk about us?"

"She was worried that if she told me who did this to her, they'd come and hurt Grace too." Amelia smiled. "She was worried about her mother too. She didn't want her to get into trouble with your father about allowing her to go to the picnic."

Tom snorted. "It was a little too late for that. Daddy beat the hell out of Mama that night."

"Daddy beat the hell out of somebody every night," Grace sneered. "It was how he was."

"Is she still here," Tom asked as he ran a hand over the swing, "or did she pass on with the funeral service at Gould's?"

"My grandmother was with Peggy when—" Amelia stopped. How could she explain Sizemore's death to them the way her grandmother had explained it to her?

"When?" Tom prodded her to reply.

"My grandmother was with Peggy when she moved from this plane to the next one," she said, leaving out any mention of Sizemore or Hodges. "She's found peace now, but I think this swing will be a sort of lifeline between where she went and here. She will be able to visit you whenever she wants to or whenever you need her to be here. The boards in this swing kept Peggy anchored to that barn all those years, but now they are here with you and can bring her home when she wants to come—the way she wanted to come for all those years."

Amelia felt the tiny hairs on the back of her neck stand up, and she turned her head to glance at the swing. In it sat the shimmering blue form of Margaret Adkins.

"She's here isn't she?" the old woman gasped as she rubbed at her arms to put the hairs flat again.

"She is," Amelia said as she stared at the smiling young face of Margaret Adkins. "Welcome home, Peggy."

Peggy stared from her sister to her brother. "They're so old."

Amelia smiled. "It's been seventy years since you've seen them."

The girl went to her sister and wrapped her in her arms. Grace shivered. "What's she doing? I feel so cold."

"She's hugging you." Amelia said. "Your aging has shocked her some."

Tom snorted. "Shocks me every time I look in the damned mirror."

Peggy released her sister and went to her brother. "He's sick," she said with tears brimming in her brown eyes. "He's going to die soon." She turned to Amelia. "May I stay with him until he does?"

"Peggy wants to know if she can stay here with the two of you for a little while."

"Of course, she can," Tom said with a broad smile. "This is her home too and she's always welcome here."

Peggy wrapped her arms around her brother, but Tom didn't give any indication of feeling her presence the way Grace had.

"There is Irish blood in the Adkins line," Jenny said into Amelia's ear. "Tom just didn't get any of the gift the way Grace did."

Amelia nodded. "You and your brother had best get back to the store. Your mother is there giving poor Nancy the third degree." Amelia pulled her phone from her pocket as though she'd received a text. "We'd better get going, Nathan," she said and motioned for her brother to move toward the door. "Mom's at the store with Nancy."

She watched the color drain from her brother's face. "Oh, good lord," he said with a sigh. "Enjoy the swing folks." He turned to Tom before opening the door. "Do you need me to help you put it up?"

The old man waved him off. "There are hooks up there where the old swing used to be. I'm not so enfeebled I can't put up a swing if the old woman will help me." He grinned over at his smiling sister.

"We'll get it up just fine, young man," Grace said, "but thank you for the kind offer." She smiled at Nathan. "You two really do look like your grandparents. You're the spitting image of Ned O'Connor, young man, and Amelia could pass for Jenny with ease."

Amelia put a hand to her head. "I'd just have to do my hair up like Miss Kitty from Gun Smoke though."

"Is Mom really at the store?" Nathan asked as they rushed toward the truck.

"Grandma popped in and gave me the news."

"I knew we shouldn't have left Nancy alone there," Nathan snapped.

Amelia rolled her eyes as she lowered the visor to block the afternoon September sun. "It's just Mother, Nathan, not armed robbers."

———

NANCY SAT TREMBLING on the display futon with Elizabeth Ryan. She put her hand protectively over her swelling belly and she hoped the loose flannel shirt she wore would hide it. Nancy had purchased her first pair of maternity jeans at Walmart the weekend before.

She hadn't expected to need them quite so soon. Everything she'd read about pregnancy said the belly bump wouldn't require more than a size or two larger than regular in the first five months but hers had grown exponentially over the last few weeks and zippered jeans were beyond uncomfortable.

"So where are my wayward children today?" Elizabeth asked as she stared around the store.

"They had to make a delivery," Nancy said.

"Do you have anything to drink around here?" Elizabeth asked.

"Amelia has soda in the fridge upstairs in her apartment." Nancy braced her hand on the arm of the sturdy futon to heft herself up. "Would you like a Coke, 7-Up, or Root Beer?"

Elizabeth patted Nancy's knee. "I can go up and get it," she said. "Those steep stairs can't be good for you in your condition."

Nancy's mouth fell open. Had Nathan already told his mother about the baby and their wedding without letting her know? They'd decided to tell his parents about her pregnancy and their wedding in Las Vegas together after the next doctor visit when Nancy would have a sonogram and hopefully get a positive sex of the baby.

They'd already settled on a girl's name. Baby girl Ryan would be called Bridget—pronounced Bree in the Celtic tradition as Nancy's due date was in early February around St. Bridget Day. They hadn't discussed boy's names at all.

The door opened, and Nathan and Amelia rushed inside. Nathan dropped onto the futon and took Nancy into his arms. "Are you all right? Where's Mom?"

"Upstairs getting a soda from the fridge," Nancy said in the comfort of her husband's arms. "How did you know she was here?"

Nathan smiled down at his wife. "Grandma popped over to give Amelia the warning."

Nancy ran a hand through her hair and sighed. "We're doomed to never have secrets in this family, aren't we?"

"Forewarned is forearmed," Nathan said then bent and kissed Nancy. "What did she want?"

Nancy shrugged. "I don't know, but she knows I'm pregnant."

"How?" Nathan asked with his eyes wide. "I didn't tell her."

"I'd better get up there to make sure the nosey witch isn't going through my underwear drawer," Amelia said and went to the stairs.

Although she wanted to stomp up the narrow wooden stairs, Amelia crept up quietly. She stopped when she heard her mother talking. Maybe she was on her cell phone. She cracked the wooden door and peeked into the apartment. Amelia gasped when she saw her mother sitting at her kitchen table in animated conversation with Jenny and Ned O'Connor.

"What the hell is going on up here, Mother?" Amelia demanded. "Can you see them?"

Ned smiled up at his gaping granddaughter. "Of course, she can see us. The gift seldom skips a generation." He patted his daughter's hand. "And my daughter has it as strong in her as her mother ever did."

Jenny sat smiling at Elizabeth and Amelia wanted to scream. "You mean to tell me you've had the ability to see the dead all this time?" she yelled at her mother. "You could see them, and yet you sent grandma to a nuthouse because she could see them?"

"Calm down, Amelia," Jenny said. "It wasn't because I could see the dead that your mother sent me away." She let out a long breath though she no longer breathed. "She sent me away because I talked about seeing the dead and that embarrassed Lizzy. Others couldn't see them and didn't think I really could either."

"But," Ned O'Connor said with a smile, "now there are reality shows on television about people who see and talk to the dead." He shrugged his shoulders.

"People are more accepting of the gift now and our Lizzy is going to be more accepting as well."

Elizabeth Ryan smiled. "I suppose I'm going to have to be with what's coming."

"What do you mean by that, Mother?" Amelia demanded. She didn't understand how her grandparents could be so understanding after everything Elizabeth had put Jenny through. She wasn't certain she could be.

"She means Nathan's little family." Ned said with a grin.

"You know about the baby?" Amelia gasped.

"I've known almost since the first time he brought that girl to the house to meet me and your father," Elizabeth said. "Those three little ones are quite chatty."

"Three?" Amelia heard Nancy gasp from behind her.

"A girl and two boys," Elizabeth said with a broad grin.

"Oh, my god," Nancy said and slumped into Nathan's arms. "Three?"

"Two boys?" Nathan asked with a grin as he patted Nancy's abdomen. "Really?"

"Over-achiever," Ned said to his grandson. "You're gonna need a house like the Sizemore Estate if you do this every time you knock her up, boy."

"Three kids are plenty," Nancy muttered, "especially if you're having them all at the same time."

"We are going to have to have a big family get-together," Elizabeth announced. "I can't wait to meet your parents, Nancy and start planning the wedding."

Amelia grinned at her brother. You're gonna have to get yourself out of that one on your own, Bubba.

Nathan had helped to ease Nancy into a chair. "Oh, my god," she said with her hands over her eyes. "How am I going to explain all of this to Mom and Dad?"

Nathan took charge of the situation. "We can have a get together, Mom," he said, "but not until next weekend after we've been to the doctor and had the sonogram." He took a deep breath and squeezed Nancy's hand. "And we're already married. We did it in Vegas two weeks ago."

Elizabeth smiled. "Then our get together will be a reception." She turned to her new daughter-in-law. "Nancy, you can put a wedding announcement in the Daily and then give me a list of everybody you would have invited to your wedding if you'd had a proper one. I'll have invitations made up and book the Mason's Hall."

Amelia smiled but felt bad for Nancy. Elizabeth Ryan was in her element and setting herself up as the family matriarch. Amelia was glad those three babies were in Nancy's belly and not hers.

It irked her that Elizabeth had treated her mother the way she had but Jenny and Ned seemed to have forgiven their daughter. Who was she to hold a grudge if they weren't?

"Mom," Amelia said, "why don't you go get Dad. Nancy, call your parents and ask them to come over here. "I'll order dinner from Applebee's to celebrate the good news about your wedding." She grinned. "Next week Mom and Dad can host the celebration of your litter."

Nancy threw her head back and groaned. "Thanks, Amelia. That's probably a good idea. I don't think they could take all the news at once."

Nathan squeezed Nancy's hand. "Two boys, Baby. We're going to have two sons."

"And they're sharing the same womb with a little girl that's very strong in the family gift," Jenny said with a giggle. "Maybe they'll absorb some of it from the amniotic fluid."

"Can you imagine three siblings running around with the gift?" Ned asked his wife.

"Not since my sisters and I," Jenny said. "Drove my parents mad."

"Oh, good lord," Nancy groaned into Nathan's shoulder.

EPILOGUE

AMELIA SAT IN THE WAITING ROOM AT THE BRIARTON Hospital along with her parents and Nancy's. Ned and Jenny hovered close by. They'd elected to put off going into the light until their great-grandchildren had been born.

Nathan was in the labor room with his wife. They heard Nancy's frequent gut-wrenching screams as the three newest Ryans made their ways into the world.

After a half hour of silence, a nurse along with Nathan came out pushing an incubator with three blanket-wrapped newborns inside. "I'd like you all to meet Bridget Jennifer, Connor Edward, and Killian Matthew Ryan," he said with a proud smile on his face. "Nancy is sleeping now but they'll have her in a room on the floor in a few minutes."

Ned and Jenny stood holding hands as they stared at the three infants. "Handsome lads, Nathan," his grandfather said. "Connor and Killian, huh?" Ned smiled. "I couldn't have come up with anything more appropriate, boy."

"Thanks, Grandpa," he whispered. "I'm glad you approve."

"Just look at all that red hair," Jenny gasped. "I bet they're all gifted."

"I'm sure they are, Jen, but I'm not waiting around another twelve or fifteen years to find out." He tugged his wife toward the glowing portal always nearby. "It's time we moved on and let these children find their own way in the world." He waved and stepped into the light. Jenny did the same with reluctance.

A tear slid down Amelia's cheek. She would miss them though it would be nice to have the apartment to herself again. She'd wakened every morning to find her grandmother sitting beside her in the bed and her grandfather sitting at the kitchen table. Amelia hadn't had much of a sex life since returning to Briarton but with the Life Shadows of her grandparents in the apartment it had been non-existent.

"Nancy said your business is going well, Nathan," Nancy's father Clifford Adams said. Clifford was a large man who wore his head shaved as many correctional officers did. He was an impressive man but didn't frighten Nathan in the least. They'd always gotten along and enjoyed going to the shooting range together.

"The store in town is doing great," Nathan said, "and Amelia's online store is still going gang-busters."

"Nancy thinks she's going to get a book deal for the barn murder story," Tonya Adams said proudly.

"And she's been getting letters from some big papers across the country," Clifford added. "It would be nice to see that Northwestern tuition finally pay off."

Nathan was aware of all of that, but he and Nancy had discussed things and she planned to remain in Briarton and write for the consortium there at least until the babies were considerably older. A book deal would allow her to stay home and that was what they were really hoping for.

They'd rented a three-bedroom house in town with a study Nancy had set up as an office. They were comfortable but that was before the birth of the babies. Nathan prayed they'd continue to be comfortable. With Amelia and Elizabeth's help, Nancy had a group of women lined up to help her with the triplets. Diapers, laundry, and formula was going to be a challenge, but Nathan and Nancy had felt lucky to have the early warning and had time to set things up for the babies ahead of time. They were thankful they didn't find out about the multiple birth at the time of delivery like so many new parents did and had months to prepare.

"They're absolutely beautiful, Nancy," Amelia said when she saw Nancy in her room, and Bridget, Connor, and Killian are perfect names. My grandparents loved them."

Nancy stretched her hand to take Amelia's. "Nathan told me they're gone now. I know you'll miss them."

Amelia giggled. "Maybe I can bring someone home now and get rid of some of this sexual tension that's been building up."

"There is that." They laughed together for several minutes like schoolgirls on a sleepover.

"Your mom says there is a big book deal in the works," Amelia said as the nurse brought in one of the babies to nurse.

"This one is Connor," she said. "We put a little dot of ink on his hand. Many parents of identicals tattoo dots somewhere on their bodies so they can tell them apart."

Nancy's eyes went wide. "Is that legal?"

The nurse giggled. "It's just a dot," she said. "Not like you're tattooing Born to Ride on one of their backsides."

"I think it's a good idea," Amelia said. "It could save you a lot of grief in the future."

"I'll talk to Nathan about it, but he'd probably opt for the Born to Ride rather than a simple dot somewhere." She put the baby to her breast and sighed as he began to ease the fullness there.

"Do you think I'm going to have enough for three?" Nancy asked the young nurse.

"Probably not," she said. "We've already started supplementing them with formula from bottles. A dietician will come and go over things with you before you all go home." She smiled at Nancy. "They really are beautiful babies, Mrs. Ryan."

"Thank you," Nancy said with her cheeks turning pink.

Nancy switched Connor to the other breast. "I can't believe they're really here," she said. "It felt like I'd been waiting forever."

"I suppose nine months can feel like forever," Amelia said, "when your belly is getting stretched every day and your bladder is being pounded from the inside."

Nancy rubbed at her rib cage. "I swear the little soccer players took turns kicking me in the ribs."

"There were three of them and they didn't have much room in there."

"What was my mom saying about my book deal?" Nancy asked with irritation in her voice. "She shouldn't be talking about my personal business like that."

"She thinks you're going to be the next Nora Roberts," Amelia said with a grin. "She and your dad are both very proud."

Nancy rolled her eyes. "Maybe if I ever see an advance check."

"Do publishers still do that?" Amelia asked as she took Connor and put him on her shoulder to burp.

"Not many," Nancy said, "but I sent out book proposals to the Big Five and I have an agent now."

"Agents do all that proposal stuff, right?"

Nancy raised a brow. "So I'm told," she said. "This one says the story about Peggy is good and will probably do well in the True Crime market, but she thinks they'll really go nuts over the story about the two little girls."

"We don't have a story yet, Nancy," Amelia said.

Nancy grinned. "But we will, sis, we will."

"We will what?" Nathan asked in a whisper as he came into the room, bent, and kissed his wife.

"Your wife is already writing the book about the two little girls in the house on Burns," Amelia said.

Connor made a loud burp and Nathan took him from Amelia. "Now, that's my boy," he said with a chuckle as he studied the infant's face. "Which boy is it?"

"That's Connor," Nancy said. "See the blue dot on his left hand between his thumb and forefinger? The nurses put it there to tell them apart and said we should think about doing it permanently, so we can too."

"Permanently?" Nathan asked with his face screwed up in confusion.

"A tattoo," Amelia said with a grin.

Nathan picked up his son's arm. "How about a

Punisher skull?" He kissed the top of the boy's red head. "You're gonna be a Punisher, aren't you, big guy?" he said in absurd baby talk.

Nancy smiled at Amelia. "What did I tell you?"

"You can probably get away with a tattooed dot, Bubba," Amelia said with a giggle, "but I think they'd throw your ass in jail for a Punisher skull."

"And rightly so," Nancy said.

The nurse brought Killian in and took Connor. "I'll bring in the little girl," she said, "and Daddy can give her a bottle."

Amelia stood. "I think I'm going to head home and leave you to your feeding."

"Get rested up, sis," Nathan said. "We finally got the permits and will start taking down the house on Burns Monday."

"That's great. What's taken so long?"

Nathan shrugged. "The house is in a residential neighborhood and some of the neighbors got up in arms about the noise the demolition was going to cause with the trucks and such, but it's all straightened out now and we can finally get the project started."

"Good," Amelia said with a yawn. "I have a few things working, but nothing concrete yet. We can use the materials from that house."

"And I can use the material for my next bestseller," Nancy said with a tired smile.

"I think we can all use some rest," Nathan said as he took Bridget into his arms and put the warm bottle of formula into her mouth.

———

NATHAN GOT into his truck to head home but wasn't as tired as he'd thought he was. He thought about stopping by the Gateway for a beer but decided against it. He had beers at home and didn't want to take a chance of getting pulled over with alcohol on his breath. Since the thing with Sheriff Tate, Nathan's bright red pickup had been pulled over more than once for bullshit offences. He didn't want to give the assholes a legitimate one.

Instead, he drove east out of town. The night was clear and the moon bright and full. It was a beautiful night for a drive and as soon as he settled down a little, he would drive home and have a celebratory beer in front of the television.

As he neared Prairie Road where his grandfather had lost his life, Nathan caught a glimpse of something odd in the mists swirling up from the river bottoms. He strained his eyes for a clearer view and his breath caught in his throat. It was a woman stumbling along the edge of the blacktop road—a woman dressed in white.

Nathan had heard the stories about the woman in white for as long as he could remember but he'd never seen her for himself. Legend had it she was the ghost of a woman who'd killed her children—or her husband and was trying to escape. Supposedly, the woman would lure a man to stop his car, beg him for a ride, and then kill him.

He knew enough about Life Shadows to be skeptical of that. She might want help, but Nathan doubted she would kill unless provoked somehow. As his truck drew closer to the spot where he'd seen the woman, the mists parted, and a woman stepped onto the pavement, waving her arms in attempt to get him to pull over.

Though he thought he was crazy for doing it, Nathan slowed his truck, pulled off into the grass, and stopped. In the side-view mirror he watched the woman jog toward the truck. She wore tight white Capri pants, a white sweater, a white scarf tied around her neck, and had a wide white headband in her dark hair. Nathan thought she looked like an actress from one of those old Elvis Presley movies.

He rolled down the window when he saw her come close.

"You need a ride, miss?" he asked. "Where's your car?"

"I need to get home," she said. "My girls are there all alone."

"Sure," he said and popped the electronic lock on the door, "climb on in."

Nathan watched the pretty young woman climb up into the truck. He guessed she was about Nancy's age—her late twenties. "I'm Nathan Ryan," he said and waited for the woman to respond.

"I'm Tammy," she said with a sultry smile and scooted closer to Nathan across the seat.

"Do you live in Briarton or out here somewhere?" She gave him an odd stare and didn't reply. "You said you needed to get home to your girls?"

"Yah," she finally said, "their daddy left them home all alone."

Nathan studied the woman. She didn't look familiar. Why was it the dad's fault the kids were home alone? She wasn't home either. Nathan didn't think the poor kids were going to have much of a chance in life with parents like these.

"Well, where do you live, and I'll get you home to your little girls."

She smiled again and scooted closer to Nathan. "You look like a nice man," she said and reached for his left hand on the steering wheel. "You're married?"

"Sure am," he said and pulled his hand away from the strange woman. "I'm just coming from the hospital where my wife gave birth to triplets tonight," he said proudly. "Two boys and a girl."

Nathan turned his head to see the woman's pretty face grow dark. "What sort of man picks up a strange woman on the side of the road after his poor wife has just gone through the pain of giving him three beautiful children?"

"A man who wanted to help a lady get home to her kids," Nathan snapped in frustration. "Now where the hell do you live, so I can take you home, Tammy whatever your name is?"

"It's Sullivan," she said and scooted back toward the door, "and I live at 1214 Burns Street in Briarton."

Recognizing the address, Nathan slammed on the brakes and pulled off the road. "Nobody lives at that address, lady," he gasped and turned his head.

Where Tammy Sullivan had been moments before, the seat was now empty. Nathan reached over to touch the leather, expecting to feel the remnants of the woman's body heat but the leather was cold to his touch. Had she been a Life Shadow? Had the two little girls Amelia had seen in that house been Tammy's little girls?

With his heart pounding in his chest, Nathan pulled the pickup back onto the highway and headed toward home. He was going to have to talk to his sister about this white lady phenomenon. If Tammy Sullivan was a Life Shadow, did it mean he was finally coming into his own as far as the family gift was concerned? Nathan wasn't certain he was too thrilled about that.

"You sure picked a great time to cross over, Grandma," Nathan mumbled as the lights of Briarton came into view.

He glanced at the time on the dashboard clock and then punched the Bluetooth feature to call Amelia. Her phone rand three times before she answered and a groggy voice. "Why the hell are you calling me after fucking midnight?"

"I just had a weird experience I can't explain, sis."

"Weird like you woke up and your cock wasn't hard, or Grandma's special kind of weird?"

"Grandma's," Nathan said with a nervous chuckle. "What can you tell me about white ladies?"

"White ladies are about all you're gonna find in Briarton except Terry, of course."

"I'm serious, Amelia. I'm talking about the white lady people see out in the bottoms."

Nathan could hear his sister sitting up in her bed. "Did you pick her up, Nathan?"

"Yep."

"And did she try to put the make on you?"

"More or less."

"Then I'm guessing you rejected her advances."

"Of course, I rejected her advances, sis. My wife just gave birth to my children tonight."

"You're lucky, Nathan. White Ladies are generally avenging spirits who seek out philandering men. Had you given her the impression you wanted to respond to her advances, you'd probably be dead in your truck right now. She'd have caused an accident that would have taken your life."

"Like the accident Grampa was in out there?" Nathan asked with his heart pounding.

Amelia didn't reply for a minute. "Grandpa was run off the road by a drunk driver, Nathan," she finally said. "I don't think your White Lady had anything to do with it. White Ladies do their thing after dark, anyhow and Grandpa's accident was in broad daylight."

"My White Lady said her name was Tammy Sullivan," Nathan said uneasily as he drove, "and that she lived at 1214 Burns Street with her two little girls."

"Oh, my lord," Amelia gasped. "Well go home and get some sleep, Bubba. You've had a long day. We'll talk about this tomorrow at the hospital with Nancy. She has a ton of notes put together on that place already and can probably add some insight."

"Thanks, sis. I just really needed to hear an objective voice. I love you."

"Good night, Bubba and I love you too," Amelia said and disconnected.

Dear reader,

We hope you enjoyed reading *Life Shadows*. Please take a moment to leave a review, even if it's a short one. Your opinion is important to us.

Discover more books by Lori Beasley Bradley at

https://www.nextchapter.pub/authors/lori-beasley-bradley

Want to know when one of our books is free or discounted? Join the newsletter at

http://eepurl.com/bqqB3H

Best regards,

Lori Beasley Bradley and the Next Chapter Team

Life Shadows
ISBN: 978-4-82410-376-5
Mass Market

Published by
Next Chapter
1-60-20 Minami-Otsuka
170-0005 Toshima-Ku, Tokyo
+818035793528

6th September 2021